ROGUE FEVER

JAN HUDSON

BANTAM BOOKS
NEW YORK · TORONTO · LONDON · SYDNEY · AUCKLAND

ROGUE FEVER

A Bantam Book / September 1995

Bantam Books are published by Bantam Books, a division of Bantam Dou-
bleday Dell Publishing Group, Inc. Its trademark, consisting of the words
"Bantam Books" and the portrayal of a rooster, is Registered in U.S. Patent
and Trademark Office and in other countries. Marca Registrada. Bantam
Books, 1540 Broadway, New York, New York 10036.

AT FIRST GLANCE HIS CASUAL POSTURE SEEMED lazy and relaxed, but after closer inspection she decided that he was about as lazy and relaxed as a coiled canebrake rattler. Instinctively, she realized that this wasn't a guy to mess with.

Savanna figured that if she had any sense, she'd turn and walk away, leave him to contemplate his beer bottle. But if she had any sense, she'd be teaching second grade instead of being in the line she was. She got a rush out of living on the edge. And the truth was, something about this fellow fascinated her. Maybe it was the big, callused hands wrapped around the beer bottle. Maybe it was the unquestionable maleness that hovered around him. Maybe it was a sense of self-preservation that nudged her forward. If she ran into trouble in Tres Lunas, this was a guy she'd want on her side.

WHAT ARE *LOVESWEPT* ROMANCES?

They are stories of true romance and touching emotion. We believe those two very important ingredients are constants in our highly sensual and very believable stories in the LOVESWEPT line. Our goal is to give you, the reader, stories of consistently high quality that may sometimes make you laugh, sometimes make you cry, but are always fresh and creative and contain many delightful surprises within their pages.

Most romance fans read an enormous number of books. Those they truly love, they keep. Others may be traded with friends and soon forgotten. We hope that each LOVESWEPT romance will be a treasure—a "keeper." We will always try to publish

LOVE STORIES YOU'LL NEVER FORGET BY AUTHORS YOU'LL ALWAYS REMEMBER

The Editors

For my editor, Beth de Guzman,
who proves that good things often
come in small packages.

With fond memories of
Elvis . . .
and special thanks to
Cora Jane Ryan, writer and
co-owner of R & R Emu Farm,
Bellville, Texas.
Any errors about the finer points
of emu husbandry are due to
author's license or my goofs.

ONE

Savanna Smith swiped the sweat trickling down her forehead from beneath her Panama hat, poked her slippery sunglasses back up on her nose, and kept a firm grip on the wheel with her left hand. Honking her horn, she dodged a bunch of squawking chickens that had escaped their pen and were pecking in the middle of the rutted, dusty road of the small Mexican village. Only her basic sense of decency had kept her from running over those blasted chickens. Lord, how she hated chickens. Chickens, turkeys, poultry of all kinds. She couldn't even abide eating the nasty things.

The Jeep, which had been new about the time she was in junior high, hit a chug hole and jarred her teeth. The wreck she drove smoked like a green brush pile and didn't possess anything that would pass for springs, but she couldn't complain. She'd bought it cheap at the border in McAllen, Texas, and made it to Tres Lunas, Mexico, using only a little over a tank of gas and almost a third of a case of oil. With any luck, she would quickly locate the plane she'd come to repossess and be rid of the clunker before it guzzled the rest of the oil. When she was ready to fly out, she would donate the Jeep and the extra oil to the local padre, who would no doubt be delighted to have it, and write it off her taxes as a charitable donation. A win/win situation.

In the small plaza, Savanna pulled up to what looked like Tres Lunas's only hotel. Two stories of plastered adobe, the Marriott, it wasn't. But she'd stayed in worse places, and she always kept insect repellent, disinfectant, and a can of Raid in her duffel bag for just such occasions. Even though she traveled light, she'd learned the hard way about certain essentials. Besides a small cosmetic kit, a couple of changes of easy-pack clothes, sandals, and extra underwear, she also carried bottled water, granola bars, and a few cans of tuna and Beanee Weenees.

Thinking of food reminded her that it was past lunchtime, but at the moment she'd settle for a shower—bugs or no bugs—and something cold to drink. Her khaki camp shirt was stuck to her back and her shorts were damp and grungy. She looked at the seedy little hotel and sighed. Air-conditioning was too much to hope for. She grabbed her shoulder bag, hoisted her duffel, and went up the steps past a dirt-yellow dog dozing in the shade. The dog didn't move except to briefly crack open one brown eye as she passed.

Come to think of it, she hadn't seen anything in the town move except for the chickens and the dog. Only the animals, wash blowing on lines behind a few houses, and colorful flowers fluttering in the plaza and in pots and planters in front of the adobe and rock buildings told her that the place was inhabited.

Inside the hotel, it was cooler. And dark. She took off her sunglasses and peered around, waiting for her eyes to adjust to the shadowy dimness. A ceiling fan stirred the air in a tiny lobby, which held only a scarred mahogany reception desk and a faded Victorian settee. A couple of fans turned lazily in a cantina situated off to one side.

She didn't see a soul around. She walked to the desk, dropped her duffel, and tapped the little silver bell on the counter. While she waited, she dug in her bag for her Spanish/English dictionary.

No one answered the ring.

She slapped the bell again and waited.

Still, no one came.

She gave it three more impatient taps.

"You can ring that damned bell from now till Christmas and it won't do you any good," a deep voice said from the direction of the cantina.

Savanna turned and squinted into the dimness. She hadn't seen the man earlier. His form only a dark outline, he sat with his chair reared back against a post, a straw cowboy hat pulled low over his brow and his booted feet crossed and resting on the table.

She took a step closer to him. "And why is that? This is a hotel, isn't it?"

"Passes for one. But Juan's gone home for a siesta."

"When will he be back?"

"Beats me. When the notion strikes him, I expect."

"Who's in charge while he's gone?"

The man took a swig of beer from his bottle and shrugged. "Nobody's in charge. Nobody's here but me, and I'm the only guest in the hotel."

"But how can I get a room?"

"You can just pick a key from behind the desk or wait until Juan gets back, but I can't imagine why you'd want a room here. The place is a dump."

She couldn't argue the point, but she didn't have much choice. "How can I get something cold to drink?"

He motioned with his head toward the bar

to his right. "Cooler behind there. The beer and the orange juice are local and good. Soft drinks and mineral water are safe. Stay away from the other bottled waters. I think Juan fills them up in the kitchen."

Savanna nodded, went to the cooler, and selected an orange juice. She opened it and took a big swig, her parched throat welcoming the refreshment. She grabbed a second bottle and walked toward the man, thinking she might be able to glean some information that would make her job easier. At least he spoke English. Maybe he would know of a landing strip nearby. She could get in, fly out, and be home before her rent was due.

She stopped a few feet from his table. He had to have heard her coming, but he didn't look up from beneath the hat brim that hid most of his face. The part that wasn't hidden was covered by a dark stubble that looked like a week's growth. His long legs remained propped on the table by one shabby boot heel. His beer bottle rested at the crotch of dusty, well-worn jeans.

His chambray shirt looked reasonably clean, but the sleeves had been ripped out at the shoulders, and she was certain that its variegated blue and white color was more apt to have come from a run-in with an errant bleach jug than a creative tie-dye bath. The shirt was unsnapped halfway down, as if the girth of his chest had popped it open. And a very nice chest it was, covered with a dark tuft of hair and as tanned as his sinewy arms.

At first glance his casual posture seemed lazy and relaxed, but after closer inspection she decided that he was about as lazy and relaxed as a coiled canebrake rattler. Instinctively, she realized that this wasn't a guy to mess with. For all she knew, he could be an escapee from Huntsville State Prison. She couldn't imagine what business an Anglo would have in this godforsaken part of the country if he weren't hiding from something. He certainly wasn't there for the tourist attractions. Except for a few orange groves, she hadn't seen anything remotely attractive for miles.

Savanna figured that if she had any sense, she'd turn and walk away, leave him to contemplate his beer bottle. But if she had any sense, she'd be teaching second grade instead of being in the line she was. She got a rush out of living on the edge. And the truth was, something about this fellow fascinated her. Maybe it was the big, callused hands wrapped around the beer bottle. Maybe it was the unquestionable maleness that hovered around him. Maybe it was a sense of self-preservation that nudged her forward. If she ran into trouble in Tres Lunas, this was a guy she'd want on her side.

She cleared her throat. "Mind if I join you?"

He glanced up and her breath caught. He had the most beautiful eyes she'd ever seen. They were a pale blue-gray, ringed with dark indigo, and they swept over her for a quick but very thorough evaluation. A slow smile, just bordering on insolence, spread over his face as his eyes continued to scan her length. Sexy didn't begin to describe this man. Virility oozed from his pores. Machismo clung to him like a second skin, formidable machismo with the quiet edge of confidence rather than the phony swaggering of a man trying to prove something.

He stood, lifted his hat, and bowed—all six feet two of him. "Delighted, ma'am," he said with what she easily identified as a Texas drawl. "Pardon my manners. I've been stuck in this place too damned long, and my mind was on other things. Please, have a seat."

Her eyebrows rose in surprise, but she sat. He repositioned his hat and sat down too. This time his boots stayed on the floor.

She sipped her juice; he swigged his Carta Blanca. He wasn't an erudite conversationalist. He seemed content to drink his beer and study her. The only expression on his face was a slight lift at one corner of his mouth, but she could read volumes from his eyes and that tiny gesture. She fought the urge to squirm and look away, but she didn't back down from his sensual scrutiny. She gave as good as she got, treating the handsome devil to the same once-over he was dishing out.

Still he didn't say a word or politely glance away, and she wouldn't. As they played their game, circling like a pair of pumas taking each other's measure, the air became charged with a crackling tension. An elemental awareness of virile male and lone female as old as the surrounding foothills sizzled across the table between them, permeated the room, and raised the temperature ten degrees.

Perspiration began to dampen her body again, but she quashed the urge to whip off her Panama and fan her feverish face. She'd sooner die than acknowledge that any man had that sort of effect on her. Besides, she didn't have time to spend on diversions or this libidinal variation of a pissing contest—especially one that seemed to be bothering her more than him.

A telltale drop of sweat trickled from beneath the brim of his hat. She laughed, mollified that she wasn't the only one affected by their potent encounter. "Hot around it, isn't it?"

With her laughter, the tension between them had receded slightly. The squint lines at the corners of his eyes deepened as he shot her a broad grin. His perfect teeth flashed white, a contrast to his darkly tanned and ruggedly handsome face. "It's only May. August is a killer."

"You come here often?"

"Nope. You?"

"Nope." She opened the second bottle of orange juice and drank from it. "You here on vacation?"

"Nope."

"Business?"

"You might say that. You?"

Savanna decided to end the parrying, to be more forthcoming and prime the pump for information from him. "I'm here for a few days to research the local flora," she said, deciding on the cover she sometimes used when she was scouting.

Deadbeats who didn't keep up the payments on their planes weren't likely to turn them over without a squawk—and some of them were very unsavory characters. Like repossessing cars, repossessing airplanes required stealth and finesse if you didn't want to get your butt shot off. And lots of detective work. The excuse of studying plants gave her license to poke around in all sorts of places. Having had a couple of botany courses in college and having been raised in the country, she knew enough to fake it.

"The local *flora*?" he asked, surprised.

"Yes. Right now I'm investigating possible

locations for a future comprehensive field study of native flora for my graduate studies in botany." She stuck out her hand. "By the way, I'm Savanna Smith."

"Ben Favor."

When his hard hand engulfed hers and a shiver slithered up her spine, she knew she'd made a mistake. Touching this man was a no-no right up there with sticking a finger in a light socket. He held on much too long, and she snatched away from his grip, fumbling for her juice bottle to cover her reaction.

"Been here long?" she asked.

"A few days."

"What kind of business are you in?"

"Ranching."

"Ah," she said, nodding. Getting information from Ben Favor was like digging a ditch with a toothpick. "You sound like you're from Texas."

"I am."

"What part?"

"Near Alvin. Ever heard of it?"

She chuckled. Two whole sentences. "Of course I have. That's Nolan Ryan's hometown. I'm from Dallas. He pitched there for a while after he left the Astros. Do you know him?"

Ben drank the last of his beer. "Yep."

Her stomach growled. "Since it doesn't look as if I'm going to get a room anytime soon, could you suggest the best place in town to eat?"

"This is it."

She looked around. "But there's nobody here to fix any food."

"Juan's wife comes in to cook. Good cook. But she already served lunch. She'll be back about six if anybody wants dinner."

Savanna sighed and pushed herself to her feet. "Looks like Beanee Weenees for me. I have some in my duffel. Want a can?"

"Thanks. I'll pass."

Ben watched Savanna as she walked away. No hip-swinging coquette this lady, but she was one hell of a sexy woman. He couldn't remember ever reacting so quickly and so viscerally to a female.

Even road-wilted and dusty she was attractive—great bone structure, nice figure, generous mouth—but he'd seen lots of women who were as physically attractive, some more so, if you liked the beauty-pageant type. He'd never gone much for the kind with the banners across their chests. He couldn't imagine Savanna Smith prancing across a stage in a bathing suit, her blond hair frizzed out into a do as big as a washtub, and simpering about world peace.

No, he had a hunch that Savanna was in a class by herself. She had something special, something that kicked him in the gut harder than a mule with his tail on fire. Maybe it was the sharpness in her eyes that could bore a hole through a man, eyes that weren't quite brown and weren't quite green but were damned seductive in their directness. Maybe it was the feisty, fearless attitude evident in her every expression. He'd bet money that this little gal was a scrapper, that she had an abundance of what his grandma used to call grit. He liked that. She was obviously independent and intelligent. He liked that too. Ben couldn't abide a clinging, dumb woman.

But something about her made him uneasy, and he couldn't quite put his finger on it. Maybe it was that she didn't fit his perception of a scientist. Try as he might, he couldn't visualize her as the studious type. Since he was going to be around for a few more days until he could grease the right palms and get his nephew Kurt out of jail, Ben decided that he would do a little research of his own.

He watched as she returned with a small can in her hand. Nice legs, he thought.

She sat down, plopped her hat on the table, and took a foil packet from her huge shoulder bag. She ripped the packet open and mopped her face, neck, and hands with the damp towelette. "I'd rather have a shower," she said when she noticed him eyeing her, "but this will have to do."

She dug in the purse, came out with a cellophane-wrapped spoon and napkin, and opened the package with her teeth.

"What all do you carry in that thing?"

"This?" she asked, patting her purse. "Oh, lots of things. I always get a couple of extra spoons when I go to the yogurt place. You never know when they'll come in handy." She popped open the can and began eating the contents with gusto. "Sure you don't want some?" she asked between bites.

"No, thanks."

When she finished, she wiped her mouth and stuffed the napkin into the can. She looked up and smiled. "Know what I'd like right now?"

He shook his head.

"A big piece of chocolate pecan pie with a scoop of Blue Bell homemade vanilla ice cream on top."

He laughed. "Sounds good, but you're not likely to get that around here."

She sighed. "Nope, not likely." She dug through her bag again and came up with a Snickers bar. "The chocolate is a little mushy, but do you want to share?"

"You go ahead."

"Think I'll save it for later." She dropped it back into the pit that was her purse.

"Think I'll have another beer. Want one?"

"No. I don't drink alcohol."

"Mind if I do?"

She smiled and shrugged. "No skin off my nose. It's your liver."

"You got that right."

Used to a lifetime with a mother and three older sisters on his back, he tended to get testy when a female censured his behavior. He strode to the cooler and grabbed another Carta Blanca. Scowling, he defiantly opened the bottle, then downed half its contents in one swig.

"Ben?"

"What?" Expecting another critical comment, he answered more sharply than he intended.

"Would you mind bringing me some mineral water on your way back?"

Rather than answer, he pulled a bottle from the cooler, walked back to the table, and plunked it down in front of her with a bang.

"Thanks," she said.

He nodded curtly and dropped down in his seat. Hooking a nearby chair with the toe of his boot, he dragged it toward him, the legs scraping noisily across the wooden floor. Deliberately ignoring Savanna Smith and her fascinating eyes, he propped his heels on the extra chair and concentrated on the rest of his beer. Instead of getting his guts in a wringer over a sexy lady, he ought to be figuring out how he could speed up his nephew's release from the local pokey.

Ignoring her wasn't easy. He heard every little sound she made—every swallow, every tiny sigh, every tap of her fingers on the table-top. He smelled her too. It wasn't sweat he smelled. It was sweet woman scent. It drifted across the few feet separating them and teased him like the tickle of a feather.

He rubbed his nose, took another long pull from his bottle. He peered at her from the corner of his eye. Hell, she wasn't paying him any attention. She was marking in some sort of book. Looked like a crossword puzzle.

She glanced up and caught him watching her. He looked away.

"What's a five-letter word for a river in Portugal?" she asked.

He shrugged. "Beats me."

She sighed. "When do you think Juan will be back?"

"Hell, I don't know," he said crossly. "Do I look like some kind of information booth?"

"No, but you're acting like some kind of jackass." She slammed down her pencil and jutted her chin. "Who stepped on your tail? I merely asked a simple, polite question. I'm dirty. I'm tired. I'd like to get a room, take a shower, and rest for a while. If I'm bothering you, Mr. Favor, I'll move and leave you to your drinking." She began gathering up her things.

His boots hit the floor, and he grabbed her

wrist. Her bones felt as delicate as a bird's in his big hand. "No. Sorry. I am acting like a jackass, but I've got a lot on my mind. Come on to the desk. We'll rustle you up a room." He grinned. "Shoot, I'll even carry your bags upstairs."

A little devil inside him had already decided which room he'd give her. The one right next to his.

Savanna stood under the spray, letting it sluice away the shampoo from her hair. The pipes rattled and groaned and the water was only tepid, but she couldn't remember when a shower had felt so glorious. She knew she ought to get dressed again and start scouting for the airstrip, but she hadn't had much sleep in the past couple of days and her muscles ached from the jarring trip in the Jeep. She was bone tired. Too tired even to dwell on Ben Favor and his hot and cold behavior downstairs. She had enough problems of her own without taking on somebody else's—even if that somebody rang her bell like crazy.

After she dried off and wrapped her hair in a towel, she delayed only long enough to wash her clothes and hang them in various areas in the bathroom before she padded to the bed and fell across the lumpy mattress.

She didn't even check for bugs.

When Ben opened the bathroom door, something wet slapped him in the face. He glanced down to the floor where the object had fallen, then picked it up and held it out by the straps. A bra. Beige and lacy. And unless he missed his guess, it was a thirty-four C. He checked the tag. Right on the money.

The door to Savanna's room was ajar, and from where he stood, he could see a long length of bare leg and the curve of a bare hip on the bed. He'd neglected to tell her that their rooms shared a bath.

If he were a gentleman, he'd discreetly close the door and go about his business.

He grinned.

Nobody had ever accused him of being a gentleman.

Ben took a step forward into Savanna's room. The board beneath his foot creaked like a rusty gate. He flinched, stilled, listened.

A soft moan, the squeak of springs, and a rustle of sheets came from the bed. He knew better than to try to sneak another peek.

He could almost hear the cackle of Grandma Katie's laughter. *Serves you right, son,* she always used to say when he invariably got caught anytime he strayed off the straight and narrow. She'd told him that he had a strong streak of rogue fever in his blood. True, he supposed. There wasn't much he hadn't tried at least once, in spite of the consequences.

But damned if he didn't have the world's worst luck. Even as a kid he always seemed to be the one who got into trouble when everybody else got off scot-free. If a baseball went through Mrs. Gillespie's window, you could bet that it had his name written on it. If a half dozen boys stole a watermelon from old man Webster's patch, it would be Ben's butt that got stung with rock salt.

The story of his life.

Ben shook his head and eased back from the open door. Looked like his bad luck was holding. Nothing new. He didn't need a conscience; fate seemed to keep a governor on his behavior. His nephew Kurt seemed to be plagued with the same curse. Poor kid. He'd have to learn the hard way to keep his nose clean.

But Ben's luck wasn't all bad. In lots of ways it was good. Too good, some might say. Like his business success. Like having a beautiful lady show up in this godforsaken place.

Still, something told him that it would take more than a stretch of dry weeds to lure a woman like Savanna to Tres Lunas. One way or another, he'd figure out what had brought her here.

He looked in the mirror, rubbed his chin, and decided that he could use a shave.

TWO

Heavenly smells of onions and spices cooking drifted through the open transom, tickled Savanna's nose, and teased her until she came slowly awake, eyelids fluttering.

Something else tickled her left forearm. Something moving slowly as if on tiny feet.

Her eyes sprang wide open. She didn't move except to lift her head slightly.

A scorpion, its tail curled over its back, crept slowly up her arm.

She muffled a gasp. Her heart kicked into high gear.

She told herself to keep still and stay calm. Beads of perspiration popped out on her forehead and upper lip. The scorpion stopped, then crawled higher. Over her elbow. Up toward her shoulder. She could feel every one of its eight little legs, and a scream built in her throat. She swallowed it down and ground her teeth together. The scream built again, pushing against her resolve with unbelievable force.

Be still. Be calm.

The hell with that!

She knocked the scorpion away at the same time a bloodcurdling scream exploded from her. Bounding from the bed, she grabbed a sneaker and a spray can from her duffel.

As the scorpion scuttled across the sheets, she shrieked and whacked it with the shoe. Once. Twice. Three times. Then she held the can at arm's length, aimed it at the creature writhing in death throes, and held down the nozzle.

There was a loud banging on the door, but she kept spraying.

The door crashed open, and Ben Favor charged in. "What's wrong?"

"Sc-sc-scorpion!" she said, pointing to the bed between them.

As he hurried over, she dropped the sneaker in her left hand, whipped the towel from her head, and held it against her breasts. When Ben bent to examine the mangled scorpion, she eased closer and peered at it. "Is it dead?" she asked, her voice still shaky.

"Deader than a doornail." His mouth twisted into a wry grin. "And I don't think it will ever be plagued with embarrassing body odor again."

"*Body odor?* What are you talking about?"

His grin widened, and he nodded toward the spray can she clutched in her hand.

Deodorant. "Oh, God." She rolled her eyes and prayed that Scotty would beam her up.

A short, dark-haired man and woman ran in, wringing their hands and speaking Spanish excitedly. Savanna said to Ben, "You explain." She grabbed her duffel and shoulder bag and beat a quick retreat to the bathroom.

She looked into the mirror and groaned. Her hair, still damp, stuck out all over her head like a wild woman's. And she was wearing only a towel and a pair of panties. Dear Lord, what Ben must think of her. Running around half nude, screaming like a blathering idiot over a scorpion, and blasting the thing with deodorant. How mortifying.

Whoa, she told herself. What did she care what some rancher from Alvin thought of her? He was a stranger, a man she'd never see again after she left Tres Lunas.

She ignored the noise and activity going on in her room while she brushed her hair dry, then caught it back with a pair of combs she unearthed from her purse.

Since the clothes she'd washed earlier were still wet, she dug through her duffel for something to wear. Her choices were limited. Jeans and a navy T-shirt, or white shorts and a pink

T-shirt. A pair of gray-blue eyes ogling her legs—and a few other places—flashed through her mind. She shook off the image, but she opted for the shorts. Not out of any consideration for Ben Favor, she told herself as she pulled on a pair of sandals. The shorts were simply cool and comfortable.

And it was not for him that she put on lipstick. Her lips were merely dry. And the perfume from a sample bottle she found stuck to a fuzzy peppermint in the bottom of her bag, why, she touched it behind her ears and between her breasts just because she liked to smell good.

Boy, she was hungry. And for something more than beans and wieners from a can. She checked her watch. It was still too early to call Rocky about checking her mail, but maybe by now Juan's wife would have dinner ready. She opened the bathroom door and peeked out.

All clear. The bed was freshly made with clean linens and the door to the hallway was closed. Before she left, she found the right can and sprayed every crack and crevice with the potent insecticide.

"Get a whiff of that, you little buggers."

Extracting a wallet with a string strap from her bigger bag, she locked her door and went downstairs.

The scrumptious scent of onions and spices grew more potent. Her mouth began to water. Following her nose, she strolled into the cantina.

Three of the tables were filled with patrons drinking beer. Locals, she supposed. One of them, a young man, ignored the conversations going on around him and watched his fingering as he softly strummed an acoustic guitar.

Ben Favor, sans hat, sat alone at the same table he'd occupied earlier. He rose as she entered. It hadn't registered earlier, but now she noticed that he'd shaved his scruffy beard. And he wore a clean white shirt and clean jeans. His dark brown hair looked newly brushed, though the wavy ends were a little shaggy over the ears and in the back. He nodded to her and smiled. Lord a-mercy, what a smile. Tom Cruise, eat your heart out.

As she strolled toward him, his eyes strayed from her face to her legs. She hated to acknowledge it, but a little thrill rushed through her. Well, truthfully, a big thrill. After all, what woman didn't like to be admired? Then she remembered that he'd seen a lot more than her legs. Her step faltered.

His smile changed to a devilish grin, and she could almost read his mind from the mischievous twinkle in his eyes. Her jaw clenched. If he teased her about the episode upstairs, she would brain him. "Don't say a word," she said. "Not a single word."

"I was only going to ask you to join me for dinner."

"Thank you. I will."

He pulled out her chair, and just as she sat down, a short Mexican man with protuberant eyes and a lush black mustache hurried over. "Señorita Smith? I am Juan Hernandez, proprietor of this humble hotel. I am so sorry about the scorpion. Mr. Favor, he explained to Maria and me what happened. Please accept my great apologies. My Maria changed the sheets, and Mr. Favor fixed the door, and we looked all over the room. No more scorpions. You have my promise."

She smiled. "Thank you. I appreciate your concern. I'm sure it will be fine."

Juan heaved a big sigh, and his look of consternation faded. "May I get something for you?"

"Just a menu."

"We have no menu. Only one dinner—like the special. But my Maria, she is a good cook. All she makes is *delicioso*."

"Then I'm sure the special will be fine."

Juan turned to Ben. "And for you, Señor Favor?"

"I'll have the special too. And a Carta Blanca."

Ben looked pointedly at Savanna after he ordered the beer, as if he were daring her to object. She didn't raise an eyebrow. It was, as

she'd told him earlier, his liver. And his choice.
She held to the principle that people could do
as they pleased as long as it didn't affect her.
Alcohol had caused a ton of misery in her life,
and she ordinarily avoided people who drank.
But she and Ben Favor were merely passing
acquaintances. While he might be the sexiest
man walking, in a day or two she'd be gone,
and she had no plans to visit Alvin.

"I like your hair down," he said. "Very
pretty."

She touched a strand at her shoulder.
"Thank you."

The silence grew awkward, his perusal
more intense. Heat flushed up her neck as she
remembered how he'd seen her dressed—or,
rather, undressed—earlier. She quickly looked
away and focused her attention on the young
man playing the guitar. "He's very good, isn't
he?"

"Uh-huh. Name's Jose. Plays with a maria-
chi band in Monterrey. He's home visiting his
mother."

"I see."

Again silence. The perusal continued. She
squirmed.

When the jovial Juan returned with their
order, she could have hugged him.

Juan busied himself unloading the tray,
serving their drinks and plates with a flourish.

Savory spice and tomato scents rose from the steaming food.

Savanna took a deep breath. "Mmmm. Smells delicious."

Juan beamed. "*Sí. Muy delicioso.*"

She recognized the beans, rice, and tortillas, but the other dish wasn't like any of the Tex-Mex food she was familiar with. "What is this?"

Juan rattled off a string of Spanish that still didn't enlighten her, then snapped open a napkin and laid it across her lap. He bowed slightly and left.

Ben grinned. "Juan used to be a waiter at an upscale restaurant in Tampico."

She picked up her fork and tasted the dish heavily laced with tomatoes, corn, cilantro, and a variety of herbs and other ingredients she didn't recognize. "Ummm. It is delicious. What did Juan call it?"

"I didn't catch it all. Something *con pollo.*"

Her stomach knotted and threatened to rebel. "*Pollo?*"

"Chicken."

Her fork clattered to her plate.

"Savanna, what's wrong?" Ben asked, sounding concerned. "You're white as a sheet."

"I can't eat chicken. I . . . uh . . . I'm allergic to chicken. And turkey. Feathered stuff. And eggs. I don't eat eggs."

"Do you need to take some kind of medicine?"

She rubbed her arms, which had broken out in chill bumps, and shook her head. "I think the bite I took was mostly tomato." She looked at the offending food on her plate and shuddered.

"Here, I'll get you something else." He took her plate and carried it to Juan, who stood behind the bar. After a few moments of conversation with the hotel owner, who grew alarmed as they spoke, Ben returned. "Maria will fix you another plate without chicken."

"Thanks. I . . . I should have mentioned it, but I'm used to having a menu."

"No problem."

She felt like such a fool. She wasn't actually allergic to chicken, but that explanation was easier than the truth. If she'd tried to eat that stuff after she found out what was in it, she'd have barfed all over the table and embarrassed herself even worse.

Savanna hadn't been able to eat anything remotely connected with chickens or turkeys since she was eleven years old. She remembered the day well. She had looked down at the heap of scrambled eggs that Aunt Emma had spooned onto her plate, felt her stomach heave, and ran for the bathroom.

First it had been eggs, then chicken, then turkey. She couldn't even bring herself to eat duck or goose or anything with feathers. As an adult she understood the reason—having to gather chicken eggs as a child had terrified her. Even now remembering some of her experiences in that dark henhouse started sweat popping out and set her heart pounding. But understanding the reason didn't make the revulsive food any more palatable.

Uncle Sid, usually when he was drunk, had taken his belt to her more than once trying to get her to eat eggs and fowl—a staple on a farm that raised turkeys and chickens. She couldn't. And neither Uncle Sid's belt on her backside nor Aunt Emma's slap across her face nor Cousin Eddie's taunting was anything new. Uncle Sid drank a lot. Aunt Emma was just plain mean. Savanna had endured their punishment for years. When she was fourteen, she'd finally become brave enough to do something about it.

Juan broke into her thoughts, uttering profuse apologies and serving her another plate of food. This time, alongside the beans and rice was a cheese tostada with pico de gallo.

"This looks wonderful, Juan. Thank you very much. And tell Maria that I'm sorry to be so much trouble."

"No problem. And while you are here, no *pollo*, no *huevos*."

"And no turkey either," Ben added.

Juan grinned. "No problem. Maria, she don't ever cook turkey."

Savanna laughed. "Good for her. Oh, Juan, I need to make a call to the States later. Is there a phone I can use?"

"*Sí.* In the office behind the stairs."

After their meal was topped off with a dessert of honey and sopapillas as light as angel wings, Savanna patted her tummy. "Maria *is* a good cook. If I stayed here very long, I'd be big as a barrel. I think I'll go make my phone call now."

Ben reared back in his chair and watched her walk away. Damn, but she was one fine female. The way he felt at the moment, and if it wasn't for Kurt—

Kurt! Oh, hell, the kid was probably starving, and here he was salivating over a woman.

Ben went to the kitchen and picked up the tray with his nephew's supper. On his way out, he passed by the office. Her back to him, Savanna laughed as she talked to someone on the phone.

"Oh, Rocky, you're a sweetheart," she purred, and Ben's step faltered. "No, no trouble. As soon as I can locate Contreras, I'm out of here."

Contreras? Ben didn't mean to eavesdrop— oh, hell, he was a liar. The minute he heard the name Contreras, his ears had perked up. He stood out of sight and strained to hear every word she said. Some of the men in the cantina started whooping it up, and he missed most of what she said, but he heard her laugh and say something about having a good cover, always getting her man, and a "quick turn-around."

Frowning, he slipped away. Contreras? Was she talking about Ricardo? He was the only Contreras around. Why would Savanna be looking for him? Something mighty fishy was going on. A cover? Why did she need a cover? Exactly who was Savanna Smith? One thing for damned sure, if she was a botanist, he was a fan dancer.

Still puzzling over what he'd heard, Ben walked across the plaza to the jail. With the toe of his boot he knocked on the thick wooden door. Pepe, wearing his usual ill-fitting uniform, opened it.

"Ah, Señor Favor."

Ben held out the tray. "For Kurt."

"*Sí*," said Pepe, who was Juan's cousin and well paid to see that Kurt got the decent food Ben or Maria brought.

"How's he doing?"

Pepe shrugged. "He is . . . *impaciente*."

"Impatient?"

"*Sí*. Impatient."

"Me too, Pepe. Me too. Any news about when your boss, the *delegado*, will be back in town?"

"Delegado Ortiz has not informed me." The jailer shrugged again. "Maybe *mañana*."

Ben's hands tightened into fists as the urge to knock Pepe's flashing gold tooth down his throat surged through him. He was getting damned sick of *mañana*. He'd been listening to that old saw for almost a week, his frustration growing daily. But losing his temper and decking what passed for a policeman in this burg wouldn't help Kurt. His nephew was already in enough trouble for a fender-bender; Ben landing in an adjoining cell wouldn't solve anything.

He uncurled his fists, said good-night to Pepe, and left. He strode to the fountain in the center of the plaza, leaned stiff-armed against the stone, and took several deep breaths. God, he'd never felt so helpless. He didn't like the feeling. He didn't like it a damned bit.

He hated being at the mercy of idiots like Delegado Ortiz and that egg-sucking Contreras, but to get Kurt released, he'd do just about anything. And that included finding out what Savanna was up to. He didn't know why she was interested in Contreras, but he wasn't about to let her do anything to screw up his plans. Contreras, with his pull and his plane and a lot of Ben's money to grease the skids, was their ticket out of this mess.

When Ben finally had his temper under control, he turned back toward the hotel. A pool of light from the cantina backlighting her, Savanna stood on the porch, watching him.

"Are you okay?" she asked.

"Yeah. Sure. I'm fine."

"You don't look fine. You look angry."

"Not angry, frustrated. Doing business with these people can wear a man down. But let's forget about that. How about a tour of the town." His chuckle was hollow. "Not that it's much of a town to see. Let's walk down this way toward the church."

They strolled down the dusty street, quiet except for the faint strains of Jose's guitar and the soft rumble of conversation in the cantina. The moon was waxing full and cast a silver sheen to the adobe and rock buildings, many lit within by a soft golden glow that spilled onto the street. Night was kind to Tres Lunas.

Lingering odors from evening meals wafted through the warm night, mixing with the earthy smells of animals and dry dirt, the gentler scents of flowers.

All in all, Savanna thought, the place might have been relaxing except for the man who walked beside her. She was excruciatingly aware of his presence. Heat radiated from his body like that of a sun-warmed boulder. She could smell his soap, his shaving lotion, the faint scent of beer on his breath, overwhelmingly masculine smells that she ordinarily didn't pay attention to.

"I like the way you smell," he said abruptly.

Savanna stumbled.

His hand went to her elbow. "Watch your step. There are lots of chug holes around here."

His hand moved from her elbow to rest lightly on her back just above her waist. She felt the imprint of his palm and the length of every finger. It seared through her cotton T-shirt and branded her skin where he touched her. She swallowed. Tried to think of something to say. Her mind was mush.

His thumb moved absently over the fastening of her bra. "What's that you're wearing?" he asked, his voice a sexy low rumble.

Her knees went watery. "Wearing?" she squeaked.

"Yes, the perfume. I like it."

"Oh, the perfume. Safari, I think."

"Sounds kind of wild." Savanna vowed that if it had that kind of effect, she'd buy a quart of the stuff when she got back to Dallas. "Safari," he said. "I'll have to remember that so I can buy Allison some."

Savanna's heart stopped cold and dropped to her stomach. "Allison? Your fiancée? Your . . . *wife?*"

"Nope. I don't have a fiancée . . . or a wife. Allison is my sister."

Her heart returned to its normal position and rhythm. "Oh, your sister."

"Yep. She has a birthday coming up soon, and she's the very devil to buy for. She's my career-woman sister."

"Career woman. As opposed to what?"

"My other two sisters don't work. That is, they work, but they have husbands and children and don't have a full-time job like Allison does. She's an advertising executive in Chicago."

Thank God. Finally she had something to talk about that would take her mind off his hand. His family. "Tell me about your other sisters."

"Well, let's see. Ellen is the oldest. She and her husband George live in Houston. He's with an oil company, and she does a lot of volunteer work. They have two kids: Kurt, who just finished his freshman year at A & M, and Karen, who's in high school.

"Then there is Meg, who plays tennis and gives a few private lessons. She's damned good too; I've never been able to beat her. She went to college on a scholarship and considered turning pro until she married Bill McKay, who's an engineer with NASA. They live in Clear Lake and have a couple of kids in junior high, Susan and Ricky, and a four-year-old we call Rip.

"And I've already told you about Allison."

"What about your parents?" Savanna asked. "Are they still living?"

"Oh, yeah. Still going strong. They have a feed store in Alvin, and my father still runs a few head of cattle. My mother has a garden every year and puts up enough vegetables for the entire clan. And she makes the best bread-and-butter pickles in Texas. I can eat a pint in one sitting. You like pickles?"

She laughed. "Yes, I like pickles. But not a pint at a time. Do you live close to your folks?"

"Yep, my land adjoins theirs. What about your family? Any brothers and sisters?"

"Nope. Just me."

"And are your parents still living?"

She shook her head. "They were killed in a car wreck when I was eight. I was asleep in the backseat and didn't get a scratch."

"Tough on you, I expect."

"Very tough."

"Who raised you?"

"I lived with an aunt and uncle for a few years, then later with a foster family," she replied, deliberately being vague. They stopped in front of the church, which was the most impressive building in Tres Lunas. Savanna looked up at the stone bell tower that rose three stories to a domed top with a cross rising from it. "This looks very old."

"It is, I imagine. Juan could probably tell you the history of it if you're interested. What happened to your aunt and uncle?"

"I don't know. I haven't seen them since I was fourteen." The subject over for her, Savanna continued walking around the plaza.

Ben fell into step beside her, and they strolled quietly for a few moments. "You don't know where they are?" he asked.

"Who?"

"Your aunt and uncle."

"No. In hell, I hope." The words were out of her mouth before she knew it. She had no intention of baring her soul to a stranger. As far as she was concerned, those six miserable years were a closed chapter in her life.

Ben let out a low whistle. "Sounds heavy."

She didn't reply. After a short silence she said, "Why is this place named Tres Lunas? Doesn't that mean 'three moons'?"

"Yes, but I don't think it has anything to do with the one in the sky. I think it has something to do with the Luna family. You might—"

"—ask Juan," she finished for him, laughing.

They had made a full circuit and were back at the hotel. "That's about it for the nighttime tour," Ben said. "There's a river just outside of town, not much of one, as you might expect, but it's better seen in daylight. Lot of snakes around these parts."

She shuddered.

"You afraid of snakes?"

"I wouldn't want one for a pet."

"Guess in your line of work you've learned to be careful of them."

"My line— Oh, yes. As I botanist, I give snakes a wide berth."

"Tell me exactly what a botanist does. I mean, when you finish your studies, what will you do?"

"Do?" She panicked momentarily, trying to come up with an answer. "I'll . . . teach."

"And perpetuate more . . . *botanists?*"

"Uh, I suppose you could put it that way."

"What school do you go to?"

"SMU," she said, automatically naming Southern Methodist University in Dallas, which she often drove by.

"Hmmm. I didn't realize that SMU had a graduate program in botany."

"It's new," she said quickly. She didn't have a clue about whether SMU had such a program or not. "I did my undergraduate study at Texas Tech." That much was true. Years before, she'd gone to Tech on a combination of scholarships and student loans. It had taken forever to pay off those loans.

As they climbed the steps, Ben's hand went

under her elbow in the automatic courtesy that she'd notice before. She hadn't needed assistance until he touched her again. Suddenly she had two left feet.

Jose was still playing the guitar; a couple of men in the cantina were doing a fair job of harmonizing to a Spanish song Savanna didn't recognize.

In the small lobby she turned and smiled up at Ben. "Thanks for the tour. Good night."

"It's early yet," he said, returning her smile with a million-megawatt one of his own. "After your nap you can't be sleepy. And there's no TV. Want to play a little Hell with me?"

Her eyes widened. She'd begun to think he was a gentleman, but the proposition he'd just made was one of the crassest she'd ever heard. And she'd heard plenty. Lifting her chin she said, "I beg your pardon?"

"I asked if you wanted to play some Hell. You know, two-handed solitaire. I'm sick of playing cards alone."

Embarrassment heated her skin. "I—I don't know how to play."

"It's easy. Do you know how to play regular solitaire?"

"Sure."

"In Hell we each have a deck and play solitaire the usual way, except that we can play on each other's aces. Game?"

"Why not?"

"Good," he said. "I'll go upstairs and get the cards. You want to find us a table and order drinks?"

"Okay with me. You want beer?"

"No, I think I'll have an orange juice," he replied with a wink.

Upstairs, Ben grabbed a deck of cards from the top of his dresser and slipped through the connecting bath to Savanna's room. He hurriedly searched her drawers, her duffel, and that big purse she lugged around. He'd never seen so much stuff crammed into such a relatively small area in his life. Her identification was obviously in the wallet she carried, and the only interesting thing he found was a small spiral notebook.

He leafed through the pages. There were all kinds of notes in a cryptic sort of shorthand, which he didn't take time to decipher and which probably made sense only to her. Then Contreras's name caught his attention. Ricardo Contreras. Damn! Beside the name was a series of letters and numbers; under it was some more chicken scratching, a phone number, and $7500.

None of it made a lick of sense. He still didn't know what she was up to. He copied the phone number, stuck the notebook back into her purse, and eased out of her room. Until he figured out what her game was, he intended to stick to her like a mustard plaster.

He chuckled to himself. That wouldn't be a hardship at all.

THREE

When Savanna awoke and looked at her travel clock, she flew out of bed. She'd forgotten to set the alarm, and she hadn't meant to sleep so late. It was after eight, and she had work to do. She and Ben had played Hell until after midnight. She'd thought that it would be a leisurely game. Wrong. It was cut-throat, took excellent hand-eye coordination, and went at breakneck speed. When she'd climbed into bed, she was so revved up that it had taken forever to drop off. She'd read a good part of the fat paperback she'd brought along before she was sleepy.

She made a quick trip to the bathroom and dressed in the clothes she'd worn the day before, planning her schedule as she went. First she needed to find the local padre and make arrangements to sign the car over to the church. Since the Mexican government took a dim view of Americans selling cars below the border, it was either abandon the old Jeep or give it away. Even though she'd need the vehicle until she located the plane, she believed in having all her ducks in a row in case she had to move quickly.

Best-case scenario: She'd spot the plane that morning and be winging her way back to Texas well before sunset.

She packed her things into the duffel and left it by the bed to take downstairs with her. She also wanted to pay Juan for her room. Three days rent ought to catch it. If she left that afternoon, the extra days would be a tip. If she ran into trouble, she was covered for another two days, which was more than enough time for almost any contingency.

Savanna made one last tour of the room and bath, checking to make sure she had all her belongings, then she hoisted her duffel and shoulder bag, grabbed her hat, and went downstairs.

Juan was sitting behind the desk, reading a newspaper. He jumped up when he saw her. "Señorita Smith! You are not leaving?"

"No, not yet." She lifted her duffel slightly. "I have my equipment in here. But I would like to go ahead and pay you for three days room and meals. Also, yesterday while you were out, I had two orange juices and a bottle of mineral water."

"Oh, Señor Favor, he already pay for the drinks."

"That was very nice of him." She glanced into the cantina but saw no one. "Is he around?"

"No. He's at the *cárcel*. He told me that you study flowers. My mother, she grows beautiful flowers. You want to see?"

Savanna smiled. "I'd love to see them later, but I study wild plants."

Juan totaled a bill for three days and handed it to her. The amount was amazingly low. She paid him from a wad of pesos she'd exchanged for at a border bank the day before.

"*Gracias*. Maria, she went home to care for the *niños*, but your breakfast is keeping warm on the stove. No *huevos*." He grinned. "Coffee, rolls—my Maria's rolls are *delicioso*—and ham. And melon. You like melon?"

"I love melon."

"*Bueno*. You sit. I'll bring."

Shortly, Juan was back with a tray of food. While he served her breakfast, Savanna asked, "Will your priest be at the church this morning?"

"Padre Alphonso? Oh, *sí*."

"Good, I'd like to talk with him. Does he speak English?"

"Very good English."

"Tell me, Juan, do you know if there is a landing strip anywhere around here?"

"A landing strip?"

"You know, where airplanes land and take off."

"Oh, *aeropuerto*. No, no *aeropuerto* in Tres Lunas. But sometimes the planes they land at Don Luna's ranch to look at the bulls. Don Luna raises very fine bulls, *toros*, for the bullfights."

"Is that the only place?"

"*Sí*. You want some orange juice?"

"Maybe later."

Juan took the tray away, and Savanna ate her breakfast. When he returned to fill her coffee cup, she asked, "Do you know if there are any airplanes at the Luna ranch now?"

He shrugged and glanced away. "Maybe. Maybe not."

"I see."

She decided that Juan was uncomfortable with her questions and didn't pursue the matter. How simple it would be if she could just straightforwardly inquire of the townspeople if anyone knew where Ricardo Contreras and his plane were. Unfortunately she'd learned the hard way that such methods didn't work, especially in small towns. As a stranger, she wasn't acquainted with the relationships—who might be a relative, a friend, or on the payroll. After a couple of bad experiences she'd learned that the best way to conduct her business was to use a clandestine approach.

One of the reasons that she was so successful at repossessions was that no one ever considered her a threat until she was airborne. Being a woman was a definite asset. She knew of two men who'd been killed repossessing planes from unsavory characters. She'd never even been shot at.

She asked Juan to fix her a box lunch, then walked outside and put on her dark glasses and hat against the glare of the sun. She spotted Ben, his back to her, standing near the fountain, talking with a wiry, nattily dressed man who wore mirrored aviator glasses and his hair in a ponytail. Deep in animated conversation, neither of the men noticed her—which was just as well. She turned in the opposite direction and walked toward the church to find the padre.

While far from being a teeming metropolis, the town was considerably more active than it had been the afternoon and evening before. She saw several people on the street and in the plaza. A couple of shops were open for business, and she lingered for a moment to admire a beautifully embroidered blue dress displayed in the window of one.

She dodged a pair of laughing, shrieking children who ran past, chasing a mangy-looking dog, smiled at their exuberance, and continued on to the church.

When she arrived, she opened the heavily carved wooden door and peered inside. Cool and dim, the interior lit only by daylight from a lovely stained glass window and myriad candles flickering at the altar, the place smelled of age, beeswax, and incense. No one sat in the wooden pews. In fact, she detected no human movement at all.

Thinking that the padre might be elsewhere on the grounds, she went around to the side of the building and through an arch in the stone wall. She found herself in an exquisite rose garden. Fragrance from the many-hued blooms filled the air. An elderly man dressed in baggy white pants and shirt and wearing a wide-brimmed straw hat knelt in the dirt, his bony shoulders hunched over, pulling weeds.

"Excuse me," Savanna said. "Uh . . . *perdone*. Uh . . . oh, rats." The man looked up, a questioning look on his weathered, wrinkled face, and she hurriedly dug through her bag for the Spanish-English dictionary.

"May I help you?" the man asked in perfect English.

"Yes, thank you. I'm looking for Father Alphonso."

"I'm Father Alphonso. You've caught me tending my roses." He stood slowly and dusted the soil from his hands. "And you are?"

"Savanna Smith. From Texas." Avoiding outright lies but skirting the truth, she told him that she was in Mexico on business, had a Jeep that she wouldn't be needing when she returned by other means in a few days, and asked if the church could use it.

He beamed. "It would be a godsend."

"You should know that it's old, not in the best of shape, and uses lots of oil, but I think it still has plenty of service left in it."

He laughed merrily. "It sounds like me. Don't worry. One of our parishioners is an excellent mechanic. Bless you for your gift."

"You might withdraw your blessing after you've bounced around in it for a few miles."

"I promise I won't. May I offer you some refreshment?"

"No, thank you. I need to be going, but here's an extra key to the Jeep. I'm not exactly sure when I'll be leaving, but if I can't deliver it to you personally, I'll send a message telling you where it can be picked up. All the paperwork will be in the glove compartment. Oh, and there'll be about a half case of oil in the back." She started to leave, then hesitated. "Father, do you have any maps of the area around Tres Lunas?"

He frowned, thinking. "Perhaps I do. Let me check." He went inside a small alcove and returned a short time later with a tattered map. "Will this do?"

She glanced at it. "Yes, thanks. May I take it? I'll leave it in the Jeep for you."

They said their good-byes, and Savanna walked back to the hotel. She noticed that Ben and the man were no longer standing by the fountain.

She found Ben inside. He sat on the Victorian settee, one booted ankle resting on the opposite knee. "Good morning."

She returned his greeting, then looked around, scanning the lobby and the cantina. "Where's Juan?"

"He had some things to take care of." He picked up a small cooler from the floor by his feet. "He left this. I had him pack some extra for me. Hope you don't mind if I join you."

Rats! Yes, she minded. Locating the plane was going to be difficult enough without Ben tagging along. He might be a sexy devil, but at the moment he was a pain in the kazoo.

"I'm sure you'd only be bored," she said. "Poking around in weeds isn't most people's idea of fun."

"Oh, I don't know. It might be kind of interesting."

She gritted her teeth. "But surely you have *business* to tend to."

"Nope. The guy I need to see is out of town." He hoisted the cooler onto his shoulder, picked up her duffel, and said, "We're burnin' daylight, ma'am." He strode out the door.

Savanna rolled her eyes heavenward and followed. It was going to be a long day.

When Ben had stowed the things in the back, he said, "Want me to drive?"

"Might as well make yourself useful." She tossed him the keys.

Behind the wheel, he said, "Which way?"

She studied the map a moment, then pointed and said, "That way."

He made a half lap around the plaza and headed west on a rutted dirt road. When they hit a chug hole, Ben exclaimed, "Good God, woman, this thing doesn't have any springs."

"My molars and my bottom are very aware of that. But if you're going to make fun of my vehicle, we can turn around right now, Mr. Favor, and you can stay in town."

"No need to get testy, darlin'. I'm going with you. I just wish I were driving my truck. At least it's comfortable."

"Where is your truck? I didn't see it at the hotel."

"That's because it's at home."

"How did you get here?"

"Flew."

Savanna's heart jolted, pounding her chest in anticipation. If he'd flown, he knew where there was a landing strip. Trying to sound casual, she said, "You flew to Tres Lunas?"

"Flew to Monterrey. I took a cab to Tres Lunas."

"A *cab*? But that's over fifty miles. Wasn't that outrageously expensive?"

"Not too bad. I cut a deal with the taxi driver. Exactly what are we looking for? What kind of . . . plants, I mean."

She did some quick improvising. "I thought that today I would just get a general idea of the area and make notes for things to examine more closely tomorrow." Digging in her bag, she came up with a pen and a small spiral notebook. She jotted in an unreadable scrawl: grass, weeds, rocks, little yellow flowers.

They drove for another three or four miles, trailing smoke. All she saw was grass, weeds, rocks, and more little yellow flowers. Now and then there was a stand of scraggly trees. Although she kept her eyes peeled, she didn't see anything that would pass for a landing strip.

"That looks interesting," Ben said, slowing and pointing.

"What?" Her mind still focused on landing strips, Savanna scanned the barren landscape. The only thing she saw where he pointed was a big clump of cacti.

"That stand of cactus. First I've seen like that. Want to stop for a closer look?"

"Sure, why not?"

He pulled over in a cloud of smoke and dust. "Bet this thing uses a lot of oil."

"Quite a bit. I probably need to check it. There's nearly a case in the back."

"You check out the cacti, I'll check the oil."

She nodded and walked over to the clump thriving on a craggy hillside. Making a few "hmmms" and trying to look interested, she looked it over and scrawled in her notebook: ll green beaver tails with big stickers. She scanned the surrounding area and didn't see anything that looked like an airstrip. There wasn't any need to go further; the terrain was becoming too rocky and hilly, and beyond were mountains. She knew the airstrip wasn't north or northwest; she'd driven in from that direction and had been on the lookout. That left south or east.

When she walked back, Ben was putting the hood down. "What did you find? Anything unusual?"

"A rather impressive stand of "—she searched her brain for something that sounded Latin—*"Cacti fideles,"* she announced triumphantly.

Ben raised his brows and looked at her strangely. He opened his mouth to say something, and she was sure that the jig was up. But he merely cleared his throat and said, "That so? I thought it was plain old prickly pear."

"That's the common name," she said quickly. She got in the Jeep and began studying the map intently. When he was back behind the wheel, she said, "There should be a road about a quarter of a mile ahead. Let's turn left, circle around, and come up from the south."

By one o'clock they were both growing hot, tired, and cross. They'd driven up and down every road and pig trail to the west and southwest of Tres Lunas. Ben had added two quarts of oil to the engine, and Savanna had examined dozens of flora that she didn't give a flip about, waxing ecstatic over plain old weeds and making up Latin names to go with them. All the while she'd scanned the area for any sign of a strip, a plane, or a hangar. Nothing.

"How about lunch now?" Ben asked.

"Fine with me."

He pulled over and parked in a grassy area beside a large tree that clung to a creek bank. They sat in the shade, and Savanna stripped off her shoes and socks, reveling in wiggling her toes while Ben unpacked the cooler.

"Hot?" he asked.

"As Hades." She fanned with her hat and held her face and neck up to the breeze.

They ate rolls and ham, sipped cool orange

juice, and listened to the buzz and drone of insects around them.

"There's a reason that the locals take a siesta about this time of day. It's too blasted hot to do anything else. Want to go back to the hotel and come back out later, when it's cooled off some?"

Savanna was tempted to say yes, but the sooner she located the plane, the sooner she could get back to Dallas and real comfort—the air-conditioned kind. "No, but I'll be happy to drop you off if you'd like," she said sweetly. She prayed that he'd take her up on the offer. She was sick to death of wasting time examining weeds.

"Nope. I'm used to working in the heat." He repositioned his hat, and she noticed that his hair was plastered to his head with perspiration. "I was just trying to make it easier on you." A bead of sweat rolled down his temple to his damp shirt collar. In fact, most of his shirt was damp with big circles and triangles of moisture.

Liar. She almost laughed at his grim expression. He was as miserable as she was.

He stood and picked up the cooler. "I'll check the oil again while you put on your shoes." He strode toward the Jeep.

She picked up a sock and gazed longingly at the lazy trickle of water in the creek, wishing she could wiggle her tired tooties in it.

Ben spat out a succinct oath.

"What's wrong?" she called.

"Flat."

She hurriedly pulled on her socks and shoes and ran to the car. Ben had the rear end jacked up and the spare out.

"I'm very sorry about this," she said.

"No big deal. I'm just glad I was along."

"I can change a tire," she said indignantly. "Move aside, and I'll show you."

He grinned. "Don't get your feathers ruffled. I'm sure you can, but why don't you let me do it this time?"

She started to argue on general principle, then thought better of it. Independent she might be; a fool she wasn't. With his muscle he could do it twice as quickly.

And very nice muscles they were, she thought as she watched them bunch and ripple across his back and arms while he wrestled the ruined tire from the axle. She'd never really understood why women went gaga over men's muscles, but watching him, she discovered that she wasn't immune to the phenomenon.

She continued to stare as he put on the spare and tightened the lug nuts. A powerful urge to run her fingers across the corded sinew and test the strength of those bulges rose up in her and tugged at her hand. She clenched her fists against the urge, but her eyes followed the rippling movements, mesmerized. She didn't understand her feelings. She didn't understand them at all. She certainly wasn't oblivious of men, but sex and the male species and romantic entanglements were way down on her list of priorities.

She'd never even been in love. Oh, there had been a couple of guys she'd been fond of, but she'd never been plagued with raging lust.

Until she'd met Ben Favor.

When he finished changing the tire and turned to her, she couldn't move. A potent awareness of his elemental maleness hung in the hot air between them. His gaze met hers, and she saw his nostrils flare.

As if in slow motion, his arm lifted and his fingers touched her face. His thumb traced a small arc under her eye.

"Oh, hell!" He jerked his hand away, popped open the snaps of his shirt, and yanked the tail from his jeans.

Her eyes widened, and a momentary panic spread over her. "What—"

"I got grease on you." Using the tail of his damp shirt, he gently wiped her face. "My hands are dirty. Sorry."

The tenderness of his actions, the male smell of his shirt, his proximity, almost overwhelmed her. She laughed nervously and stepped back. "I've had grease on me before. Don't worry about it. Are we ready to go?"

"We've got a little problem."

"What?"

"The spare is low, and its tread is paper-thin. It might hold until we get back to Tres Lunas, but it's not safe to be riding around on. We'll have to get the tire fixed and see if we can round up another spare. You don't want to be caught in these parts without a good spare."

She sighed. "It looks like we'll get that siesta after all."

"Sorry."

She shrugged. "It's just one of those things." She grinned. "Anyhow, I'd love a shower right now."

A mischievous twinkle lit his eyes. "Me too. Want to share?"

"Ben Favor!"

"Is that a no?"

Savanna stood under the cool spray, letting the water sluice away the soap and shampoo and thinking that it was pure heaven. Ben, bless him, had insisted on tending to the tire repair and had dropped her off at the hotel with her gear. Her protests had been half-hearted at best.

After she'd dried off and washed her clothes, she went into her bedroom to dress again. As she pulled on her panties, she remembered that it was siesta time, and she knew that nothing short of a miracle would have the tire repaired before evening at least. Then it would be too late to go out looking again. Damn!

After she shook her sheets to roust any hidden creepy-crawlers, she sprayed a ring of insecticide around the bed, then flopped down on the mattress. She put her hands behind her head, stared up at the droning ceiling fan, and cursed her luck.

Ben strode into his room, tossed his hat on the dresser, and ripped off his sweaty shirt. He was blistering hot, and trying to deal with that guy at the garage had steamed him up even more. He sat on the bed and yanked off his boots, stood, and peeled off his jeans. All he could think about was a shower.

He crossed to the bathroom door, then hesitated as his hand touched the knob. God, Savanna would have a fit if he walked in on her. He put his ear to the door and listened. All quiet.

He eased the door open and peeked inside. All clear except for her laundry. But her door to the bathroom stood open, and he could see her bare legs on the bed. Long and smooth and lovely. Enticing. Damned enticing.

He felt like a kid eyeing a cookie jar.

His feet took one step, then another, then another until he found himself beside her bed.

Her back was to him. It was flawless except for a small flat mole on her left shoulder blade. His gaze followed the curve of her body over the dip of her waist and the swell of her hip. Another tiny mole. This one was at the top edge of her lacy panties. They were blue, bikini-cut, and had the delicate patina of silk. He wondered if they were as soft as they looked. He wondered if *she* was as soft as she looked.

His fingers reached out and hovered an inch from her skin.

Fool! He jerked his hand back.

He stood there for the longest time, almost salivating and wanting nothing as badly as he wanted to climb into that bed with her.

Dammit! Get ahold of yourself, man.

He told himself that he should leave, but his feet felt nailed to the floor. He cursed himself for being a voyeur, told himself that he was acting like a randy teenager. The randy part was true for sure. And he hadn't even kissed her. But he wanted to. God, how he wanted to.

But not like this. He wanted her wide awake.

He spotted her purse beside the bed. Now was a good time to check her ID. Just because he had the hots for her didn't mean that he trusted her one iota. He still wanted to know what her game was. Before he'd come upstairs he'd called the number he'd found by Con-

treras's name. It was a Dallas bank. Which told
him zilch. But it did make him wonder about a
connection among Savanna, Contreras, and a
bank.

Contreras was such a slimy little slug that
Ben wouldn't be surprised to find out that he'd
robbed a bank or was peddling dope and laun-
dering money. If Savanna was using a cover,
she could be some kind of law enforcement
agent on Contreras's tail. Or for all he knew,
she could be trying to make a buy. Naw, he
couldn't see her as a druggy. But he couldn't
see her as the law either. There was one way to
find out.

Just as he reached for her purse, she
groaned and stretched. He jerked his hand
away, quietly backed out of the room, and
eased her door shut. If she caught him rifling
her purse, there would be hell to pay.

He stepped into the shower and turned the
cold water on full force. It didn't help much. It
was only lukewarm.

Who in the hell was Savanna Smith? And
what was it about her that had him tied in
knots? He'd had his share of women—tall
ones, short ones, blondes and brunettes and
redheads with varying degrees of pulchritude,
and he'd *never* had one ring his bell like Savanna. He was beginning to understand the
term *obsession*. Even knowing that her tale
about being a botanist was a crock and that she

could put a major kink in his plans, she was all he could think about.

As he lathered his hair and body, her image swam in his mind. Not just the bare skin he'd seen or the swell of her hips. Her eyes. Her lips—their shape, their animation, their smile.

He was going to taste those lips before the night was over.

FOUR

The low drone of an insect brought Savanna to the edge of consciousness. She shifted restlessly. The droning continued. Loudly. Steadily. Not like a fly or a mosquito, the sound was more like—

She shot up, wide-awake.

A plane!

Bounding from the bed, she ran to the street side of her room, batted aside the curtains, and threw open a window. Leaning out as far as she could, she shaded her eyes and scanned the sky.

There it was! A blue and white single engine headed east. She watched until it disappeared from sight, but she was almost sure that it was coming in for a landing somewhere out there. While she couldn't read its identifying numbers, she'd bet anything that the plane she'd spotted was the Cessna she'd come to find.

Gotcha!

Suddenly it occurred to her that she was hanging out the window, practically nude, bare boobs in plain view of the entire town. Quickly she looked around below. She saw only one person. A pudgy man dressed in an ill-fitting khaki uniform stood near the fountain, grinning up at her.

His grin widened, and he tipped his cap.

She glared at him. "Pervert!" she yelled, then slammed down the window.

If she'd had time to dwell on it, she might have been embarrassed, but she didn't have time. All she could think of was getting dressed and locating that plane. Pronto!

She dashed for the bathroom, yanked open the door, and slammed smack into a large, un-clad chest. She let out a shriek that could have raised the dead and tried to jump back, but strong hands gripped her forearms.

"Whoa," he said.

Her eyes growing as big as flour tortillas, she looked up into the amused face of Ben Favor.

"What are *you* doing in here?" she demanded.

"Oh, the usual things one does in a bathroom. I just got out of the shower."

Instantly she became aware that her hands

were on his shoulders, her breasts were pressed against his chest, and other parts of her were also in very close contact. She felt the dampness of his body and felt it seep into the silk of her panties.

Her brain went completely haywire. She knew she should move away from him, tried to move, in fact, but the messages didn't seem to make it to her muscles.

The feeling of her dry body against his warm, wet one was extremely . . . pleasant.

Sensual.

Erotic.

She tried to say something. Licked her lips, opened her mouth, and looked up at him. Every synapse in her speech center melted.

His pupils had become wide black eddies of longing, dark, magnetic abysses that pulled her into their depths. Strong currents of desire charged the air around them, quivered in the space between his lips and hers.

"I have to kiss you," he said, his voice husky as he slowly lowered his mouth toward hers.

"I know," she murmured with a breathy sigh.

His lips were warm and wet, fevered in their capture of hers, but soft. Oh, so soft. He groaned and thrust with his tongue. She moaned and met his thrust with one of her own.

His mouth moved over hers with fervid hunger; she returned his onslaught with a matching fervor. Passion sparked, flamed, and spread like wildfire.

His hands pressed her closer as they slid down her back, cupped her buttocks, and ground her against him. She could feel his hardness, and a deep, answering ache throbbed low in her body. She whimpered and writhed against him, her hands clutching his back, her knee rubbing his flank.

He tore his mouth away and groaned. With a swift movement he swept her up into his arms.

Her heart fluttered. "What are you doing?"

"Unless you want it right here on the floor, I'm taking you to bed."

A bucket of ice water couldn't have sobered her more than his indelicate words. She stiffened in his arms. "Put me down. Right here. Right now."

He hesitated only a moment, then set her on her feet. He scanned her face, a perplexed look on his own. "Was I reading the signals wrong?"

She raised her chin and glared at him. "I don't know what signals you were reading, but I'm not in the habit of hopping into bed with virtual strangers. How dare you sneak into my bathroom and try to seduce me!"

"Now, wait just a damned minute! In the first place, I didn't sneak anywhere. This is my bathroom too. And *seduce* you? Hell, Savanna, you were hot to trot and climbing all over me."

"Hot to trot? Climbing all over you?" She stuck her hands on her hips and shot daggers at him. "In your dreams, Ben Favor. Now, get the hell out of my bathroom and put your pants on! I have to get dressed."

"I told you, it's not *your* bathroom. It's *our* bathroom, and I'm staying. Where are you going?"

"To study plants, of course. That's why I'm here." She kept her eyes firmly on his Adam's apple, daring not to look down. A quick peek a second before had almost sent her into orbit. He was still fully and magnificently aroused. His nudity didn't seem to bother him in the least.

He made a strangled sound. When her gaze traveled from his throat to his face, she found that he was staring at her breasts. Automatically, her arm started to move to cover herself. She forced it back down. Ordinarily a modest person, she would have died before she would capitulate to this man. To any man. Two could play his game. She squared her shoulders and stood her ground, daring her nipples to betray her.

Despite her determination, she felt the recalcitrant areolas pucker beneath his scrutiny. When she heard his low chuckle, she said haughtily, "It's chilly in here. Excuse me, I need to brush my teeth." She strode past him to the basin and grabbed her toothbrush.

"Darlin', despite the thick adobe walls, it's at least eighty degrees in here. And getting hotter by the minute."

She held her brush in a death grip to keep her fingers from trembling and squirted a blue blob of toothpaste on the bristles. The blob, which was twice as much as she needed, promptly slid off and plopped into the sink. She propped herself, stiff-armed and head down, against the basin. "Aren't you going to be a gentleman and leave?"

"I've never claimed to be a gentleman. I think I'll stay and watch."

"What are you? Some kind of Peeping Tom?" She glared at him as he casually leaned against the doorjamb, one hand on his out-slung hip. The hair on his broad chest had dried into a curly dark mass that thinned to trail down to a darker thatch—

Horrified at the path her gaze had taken, she quickly turned her attention to her tooth-brush.

"Takes one to know one," he told her.

She scraped the toothpaste onto her brush and began vigorously brushing her teeth. She didn't realize what was happening until she heard a quick indrawn breath from Ben. Continuing to brush, she glanced at him and then down at her breasts. Some perverse sense of one-upmanship prevented her from giving in to her mortification and ending the wiggle-and-jiggle exhibition.

Her teeth had never been so clean.

When she had finished, she stuck her brush in a glass and turned to him. Though he tried to act blasé, a sheen of perspiration coated his upper lip. She also noticed that he'd knotted a towel around his waist.

She looked pointedly at the towel, then up at him. Cocking one eyebrow, she asked sarcastically, "Did you get chilly?"

"Hardly."

She rolled her eyes. "Well, the bathroom's all yours now. I'm going to get dressed."

"And go where?"

"I told you. To look for plants."

"How?"

"In the—" She frowned. "You didn't get the tire fixed?"

"I had to leave the Jeep at the garage. The guy there said he would get to it as soon as he could."

"When will that be?"

"*¿Quien sabe?* Who knows? I wouldn't count on it until tomorrow morning at least."

"I don't suppose there's a car around here that I could rent?"

He snorted. "In Tres Lunas? Not likely."

She made a disgruntled noise. "What am I going to do now?" she muttered.

A slow smile lifted one corner of his mouth. "We could play some Hell."

She uttered a succinct and very rude phrase, stomped out, and slammed the bathroom door. His hoot of laughter echoed behind her.

Muttering vile oaths about Ben Favor's ancestry, Savanna pawed through her duffel for clean underwear, her white shorts, and the pink T-shirt. She dressed quickly, disdaining even a drop of perfume or a touch of lipstick. With the possible exception of her drunken uncle Sid and that contemptible piece of trash that was his son, never had a man infuriated her so much as Ben Favor. Certainly no one in recent years.

She grabbed her paperback novel, piled pillows against the headboard, and plopped down to read.

But she was too restless to read. The scene in the bathroom replayed over and over in her head. She had never in her life acted as she had with Ben. And the ugly truth was that she wasn't nearly as furious with him as she was with herself. Furious and thoroughly disgusted.

She tossed the book aside.

Another ugly truth was that she *had* been

climbing all over him. Without even trying he'd lit fires in her as no man ever had done. She'd been only a hairbreadth away from going to bed with someone who was practically a stranger. Very unlike her. Savanna Smith was cool, calm, and collected. The ice queen, she'd been called.

She rested her forehead on her bent knees and wrapped her arms around her head, wishing with all her might that she could turn the clock back and erase the entire humiliating episode. Dear Lord, had she actually stayed in that bathroom with a naked man, and her in nothing but damp panties? She'd never pulled such a stupid stunt in her life. What had possessed her?

The sooner she located that plane and got away from this place, the better off she'd be. If she hung around much longer, the ice queen would be nothing but a warm puddle.

One sock on and the other dangling from his fingers, Ben sat on the side of his bed, cursing himself for seven kinds of fool. He'd handled the situation badly. He knew that. Hell, growing up with three sisters, he probably understood women better than most men— which wasn't saying that he didn't have a long way to go.

He couldn't count how many times one of

his sisters, usually Allison, had looked down her nose at him as if he were a bug and said, "Ben, don't be *crude*." That's what he'd been with Savanna. Crude.

He knew better. His hormones had over-ridden his good sense—which was no excuse. Women, no matter how independent and sassy, liked to be treated with a little finesse. He'd treated Savanna with all the finesse of a frenzied bull elephant at estrus. Hell, when he'd kissed her and she'd responded the way she had, he'd *felt* like a frenzied bull elephant.

Despite her efforts to brazen it out—a damned good job, which might have fooled most men—he realized that he'd embarrassed her, humiliated her, then rubbed salt in the wound. Hell, standing around buck naked and ready, ogling her breasts—what had gotten into him?

He thought of that old saw *The devil made me do it*, which was near enough to the truth. The very grit and toe-to-toe tenacity that he admired in Savanna also roused his competi-tive nature, made him itch to take her down a peg. That and the fact that she turned him on without even trying, made him want to beat his chest and shout "Me Tarzan, you Jane."

Oh, hell. Why was he getting his shorts in a wad over a woman he'd just met and proba-bly would never see again after he left Tres Lunas? She was trouble with a capital T, and he already had plenty of trouble on his plate without an extra helping. He'd be smarter to spend his time figuring out her connection to Contreras and keep her from screwing up his deal than figuring out how to get her into his bed.

He pulled on his other sock and his boots, then stood.

Who was he kidding? He wasn't through with Savanna Smith by a long shot. He was just going to have to tread a little more carefully, keep his hands in his pockets and his pants on. And his eyes open. Maybe he was asking for a double dose of trouble, but no law said he couldn't romance the lady a little while he was keeping an eye on her.

Hell, Trouble was his middle name.

Savanna stayed in her room until hunger and the smells wafting up from below almost drove her crazy. The bout with the scorpion one day before had been bad enough—at least she'd covered herself with the towel after he broke into her room—but she didn't know how she would be able to face Ben after the latest episode in the bathroom.

No, that wasn't true. She knew exactly how she'd handle it. She would hold her head up and pretend it never happened and dare Ben Favor to so much as twitch his lips. In lieu of armor, she changed into her jeans and long-sleeved navy T-shirt and started downstairs. With every step she took, her resolve grew.

By the time she entered the cantina, her backbone was stiff and her jaws ached with determination.

The place looked much as it had the evening before: three tables of locals drinking beer, Jose strumming his guitar. Her gaze went automatically to Ben's table.

It was empty. She relaxed.

Juan came rushing over, smiling and affable as always. "Ah, Señorita Smith." He ushered her in and held her chair as she sat down in her usual place. "You wish to eat now?"

"In a moment. I'd like to ask you about something first. This afternoon I noticed a small airplane heading east from town."

"¿Sí?"

"What is east of town?"

"Don Luna's ranch. It has many, many acres."

"Could the plane have been going there?"

He shrugged again. "I don't know. Maybe."

"Any idea who the plane belongs to?"

He shrugged. "Maybe Don Luna's—how do you say?—the husband of his daughter. You wish to eat now? My Maria, she fix a very fine roast beef for you. You like roast beef?"

"I love roast beef. And may I have some mineral water?"

He beamed and left quickly, which was just as well. She'd broken one of her cardinal rules—asking too many curious questions, especially of the same person. And especially when he seemed to be uncomfortable about it. Why was Juan so obviously uncomfortable? She'd bet that the plane *had* landed at Don Luna's ranch. Was Juan's reticence a natural awe of the local bigwig, or was there something fishy going on at that ranch? And who exactly was Don Luna's son-in-law?

Tomorrow she would find a way to check out the ranch. *If* the Jeep's tires were repaired.

Ben Favor and Juan appeared at the table at the same time. She ignored Ben. To Juan she said, *"Gracias"* as he set her mineral water before her.

"De nada," he responded graciously. "You would like your dinner now, Señor Favor?"

"Please." Ben turned to Savanna. "May I join you?"

"Certainly." What else could she say?

He hung his hat on the back of a chair, pulled out another, and sat down across from her.

For what seemed like an eternity, neither of them said a word. Not daring to look at Ben, she watched Jose's fingers deftly strum his guitar. When she realized that she was nervously twirling her water round and round, she froze, then casually lifted it and took a sip.

The silence stretched interminably. Where was Juan with their food?

"Uh, how about them Cowboys?" he said.

She glanced at him. His expression was solemn. If he'd been smirking, she would have beaned him with her bottle.

Their gazes met briefly, then slid away, then met again. The scene in the bathroom flashed through her mind. Time and distance had given her a slightly different perspective. Now it seemed funny.

Her lips twitched. A bubble of laughter built in her throat, worked its way upward, and exploded. He grinned and started laughing too.

"I'm sorry about that," he said.

"Me too. Let's forget it."

"Good idea."

Juan served their food, and while they ate they fell into an easy conversation about casual subjects.

"By the way," Ben said, "I checked on the tire. The guy at the garage said that he'd have it ready by midmorning. He has one that might do for a spare as well."

"Great. Thanks. I need to get on with my research."

Even though they'd agreed to forget about the scene in the bathroom and continued to

make small talk, the sensual awareness remained there, sizzling a millimeter beneath
the surface. The deep timbre of his voice re-
verberated inside her; his rugged presence sent
ripples of awareness over her skin. She became
fascinated with his mouth as he spoke, remembering—

Suddenly she couldn't breathe properly.

She pushed away from the table abruptly
and stood. "I'm going for a walk."

Ben tossed his napkin aside. "I'll come
with you."

"I—I'd rather you didn't." She turned and
hurried away.

Outside, she drew big lungfuls of air, trying to clear her head and still the beehive inside her. What was it about that man that
affected her so? He was good-looking, but
she'd met dozens of men who were handsome
—a few even more so than he was. But there
was something special about Ben. They
seemed to connect at some deep level that she
didn't understand.

She began walking at a fast clip, ending up
at the church. Father Alphonso, in his robes,
stood on the steps talking to a small group as
they made their departure. Seeing him gave
her an idea. Savanna hung back, waiting until
he was alone.

When he'd waved to the last person, she
stepped forward. "Good evening, Father."

"Ah, Miss Smith. Good evening. Is the map helpful in your research?"

"Yes, very much so. Thank you. I have some questions I'd like to ask if you have a moment."

"Surely."

"I understand that most of the land to the east belongs to Don Luna. Is he a member of your parish?"

"Oh, yes. He is very generous to our church and employs many of our people."

"I've been told that he raises bulls for the bullrings."

"Yes, very fine ones, I'm told. I don't know much of such things, but it has been a tradition in the Luna family for many, many years."

"I, uh, find the idea fascinating, and I was wondering if Don Luna would possibly allow me to tour his ranch, see the bulls, and perhaps note the flora there."

"Don Luna is very gracious. I'm sure that he would, but he is away on business for several days. In fact, he left just this morning."

Disappointed, she said, "I see. Well, it was just a thought I had. Good night, Father."

"*¡Buenas noches!*"

Rats! she thought as she walked back to the hotel. So much for that bright idea. She kicked at a rock in her path. She'd have to find another way to scout the ranch.

As she neared the hotel, a figure stepped out of the shadows and her heart jolted.

"Savanna?"

"Ben? You startled me."

"Sorry." He fell into step beside her. "I just didn't like the idea of you being out there alone."

"I'm perfectly capable of taking care of myself. I've been doing it for a long time."

When they started up the steps, his hand touched her back lightly. She flinched as if she'd been burned.

"Savanna, I think we need to talk."

"But we've been talking all evening."

"No, I mean really talk."

"About what?" she asked.

"About this thing that's happening between us."

"What thing? I don't have the vaguest notion of what you mean. Now, if you'll excuse me, I'm going to my room. Good night."

He caught her before she fled and turned her to face him. He brushed his lips against hers, briefly, gently, and she felt a flash of current tingle through her.

"This thing," he murmured against her mouth. "This thing."

FIVE

Savanna's butt was dragging when she came down to breakfast. She hadn't slept worth a darn. She'd tried counting backward from a hundred several times. Ben's image kept popping up and making her lose count.

She'd lied to him the night before about not knowing that something was happening between them. She knew exactly what he meant. Something potent boiled between them, something beyond her control.

And Savanna didn't like losing control. She didn't like it a bit.

After she'd worked up the gumption to report her abusive relatives to the school counselor when she was fourteen, she'd been determined to hold the reins to her life. Reporting her aunt and uncle and that slimy cousin was the smartest thing she ever did.

Since then, she hadn't backed down or allowed herself to be cowed by anyone or anything.

The best thing that had happened in her young life was being placed with her foster parents, Don and Nancy Malmquist, a warm, wonderful couple whose children were grown and gone. Don had been a retired airline pilot who wisely recognized Savanna's battered self-esteem and need for control. He'd taught her to fly when she was fifteen. That had been the second best thing that ever happened to her. Flying became her passion, the day when she'd own her own plane a burning dream.

And that was why she was in Tres Lunas, dammit. To pay the rent and sock away another chunk in the plane fund. She wasn't in Mexico to get jazzed up over a sexy Texas cowboy.

Her resolve renewed, she looked around for Juan. He wasn't in the lobby or the cantina. She poked her head out the front door and found him sweeping the steps.

"Ah, *buenos días*, Señorita Smith. Are you ready for your breakfast? Señor Favor, he already ate."

Her gaze followed his gesture toward the plaza fountain. Ben stood talking to the same wiry man with the ponytail she'd seen him with the day before. A red Corvette was parked nearby.

"In a moment, Juan," she said distractedly,

keeping her attention on the two across the way. "Who's that man that Ben is talking to?"

Juan frowned, then said, "Ricardo is Don Luna's *yerno*, the husband of Don Luna's daughter."

Her heart lurched with anticipation, but she forced herself to remain calm and cool. "Ricardo . . . ?"

"Ricardo Contreras."

Bingo!

"You want your breakfast now?"

"Later, Juan."

Her eyes narrowed as she watched the two men. What was Ben talking to Contreras about? Why were they so buddy-buddy? She couldn't imagine what business a rancher would have with Contreras. For that matter, she couldn't imagine what business a rancher would have in Tres Lunas. The only cattle around the area were fighting bulls. Come to think of it, Ben had been very evasive about his business in the town. Every time she brought the subject up, he changed it.

What if he weren't a rancher after all?

But what else could he be? What was he after with Contreras?

With Ricardo Contreras's history, Ben could be a crook in league with him or a lawman on his tail. Or—

Or, by gum, he could be in the same line she was. Wouldn't that be a kicker? The friend who'd clued her in about looking for Ricardo in Tres Lunas had said that a tall man had been nosing around the private airport where he worked a couple of days before. Her friend hadn't told him anything, but—

Naw, she thought, she didn't see Ben as a repo man. Besides, she knew most of the people who worked airplane repossessions. There weren't many of them. Still, she was going to stay on her toes. The sooner she located that Cessna and got away, the better.

A plan formed quickly in her mind. If it worked, she'd be in Texas before dinnertime. She tucked her pink T-shirt into her shorts so that it molded her breasts, threw back her shoulders, and sauntered toward the fountain, adding a swing to her hips and pasting a huge smile across her face.

Ben saw her first and stopped in midsentence to gape at her. Ricardo turned and spotted her. Both men watched her approach with frank admiration.

"Good morning," she said to Ben.

Grinning, he tipped his straw hat. "Morning."

She turned to Ricardo and jacked her smile up another notch. "Ben, aren't you going to introduce me to your handsome friend?"

Ricardo, who wore a plethora of gold chains in the neck of his gray silk shirt, was blatantly studying her cleavage. Beneath his thick mustache, his thin lips stretched into an oily smile.

"Savanna Smith, Ricardo Contreras," Ben said gruffly.

"So pleased to meet you." She held out her hand, took his offered one between the two of hers, and squeezed. "Or should I say *'buenos días'*? Do you speak English? My Spanish is just terrible." She patted his hand and held on to it.

He managed to drag his concentration from her bosom to her face. "I speak English."

"Well, isn't that wonderful. From what I've heard, I'll bet that you were the one flying that plane I saw yesterday. I just *love* cute little airplanes like that one. They're sooooo exciting," she simpered, fluttering her eyelashes. Ben made a strangled sound. She ignored him. "Is it yours?"

Ricardo's thin chest puffed out, and his grin broadened into a swaggering parody of machismo. "Yes, the plane is mine."

"Oh, how divine! I'd love to go up for a ride and see the countryside." She cocked her head, batted her eyelashes again, and smiled sweetly. "Is it possible that you could take me up in your plane today?" She squeezed his hand again. She considered twirling one of his gold neck chains around her finger but decided that was a little much.

"Today is impossible," he said, looking sincerely crestfallen. "I am on my way to Monterrey on business. But I'll return tomorrow morning. I will stop by and take you then."

"Oh, how wonderful!" she squealed. "Isn't that wonderful, Ben?"

Ben looked as if he'd just stepped into something gross. "Just hunky-dory." He nodded to Ricardo, grabbed Savanna's arm, and said gruffly, "Let's go."

"*¡Buenos días!*" she called brightly over her shoulder to Ricardo as Ben dragged her away. "I'll see you tomorrow."

Ben marched her across the plaza and into the hotel. Once inside, she said, "Let go of me," and shook off his hold. "And stop glaring at me."

His hands on his hips, Ben continued to glare. "You want to tell me what the hell that was about?"

"What?"

"Oh, I just *love* cute little airplanes," he simpered in a falsetto.

She stuck her nose in the air. "Well, I do."

He made a disgusted snort. "Savanna, the man is married, and his wife is eight months pregnant."

"So?"

"Anything you want from Ricardo Contreras, you can get from me."

Her gaze flicked over his length from

boots to hat, and she cocked one eyebrow. "You have an airplane?"

He spat out a succinct sibilant oath, turned on his heel, and stomped off.

Good enough for him, she thought, turning and stomping off in the opposite direction. Lord, men could be such pains in the butt. Ben didn't have any idea why she'd fawned all over Ricardo, and she wasn't about to tell him that pandering to the oily little weasel's ego was a carefully calculated act. Unless she was lucky and located the plane that day and could make off with it before he returned from Monterrey, flying with Ricardo was the best way to find out exactly where the Cessna and the landing strip were. Her pocketbook was growing dangerously thin, and returning the plane to the bank where it had been financed would fatten it by several thousand dollars.

Ben muttered all the way to the garage. He still didn't know what Savanna was up to, but he didn't believe that Contreras had known her before a few minutes ago. What was that act she pulled? He'd wanted to smash Contreras's face in for ogling her. Not that he was jealous.

Dammit! Yes, he was jealous. Savanna had burrowed under his skin more than he wanted to admit.

And he'd landed in a hell of a quandary.

One thing for sure—he wasn't about to let her out of his sight for a minute.

After breakfast Savanna asked Juan where the local garage was. The directions were simple. Hoisting her gear, she went out the front door of the hotel.

The Jeep was parked in front. Ben Favor leaned against the hood. "You ready to scout for weeds?"

"I'm going to study the flora east of here, if that's what you mean. Thank you very much for having the tire repaired." She reached into her purse. "How much was the bill?"

"Not much. Forget it."

"I insist on paying my way."

"Insist all you want. It's already taken care of. Wait here, and I'll get our lunch."

She made a face at his back. "In your dreams, Ben Favor. I'm out of here." She tossed her stuff into the Jeep, scrambled in, and reached for the ignition.

No key.

She glanced toward the hotel. His hat pushed back, Ben leaned against the doorjamb, grinning and dangling the key chain.

Savanna crossed her arms and fumed until he returned with a large cooler.

He stowed the cooler in the back, came to

the driver's side, where she sat, and said, "Move over."

"I'm not moving. Give me the key."

"Nope."

"If I'm forced to, I'll hot-wire this sucker." She bent under the dash.

"Damned stubborn woman!" He stomped around to the driver's side and got in. "Here." He slapped the key into her hand.

"Thank you," she said, giving him a phony smile. "And since you seem to have such a low opinion of my project, perhaps you should stay here."

"I'm going."

Since he looked dug in for the duration, she cranked up the Jeep and headed east. Talk about stubborn!

Talk about stubborn! Ben thought. Trying to court Savanna was like trying to pet a porcupine. And that was exactly what he'd planned to do—court her. He'd keep her occupied and divert her from Contreras. His plan called for old-fashioned hands-off wooing. He'd intended to charm the pants off her—figuratively speaking. Well, maybe literally would be nice too, he thought.

He'd had Maria fix up a special picnic lunch, complete with tablecloth and napkins, and had made arrangements for a romantic candlelight dinner that night in a private little courtyard behind the hotel. Hell, he'd even paid Jose to serenade her.

But it was damned hard to pursue a woman who, despite her tendency to run around in nothing but a pair of panties, had more armor than an armadillo and was pricklier than a cactus pad. And it hadn't helped his plans any when she'd slobbered all over that jerk-off Ricardo. Hell, she'd done everything except unzip that banty rooster's pants. Ricardo was a sleazeball. If Ben hadn't been forced to do business with him, he wouldn't have given Ricardo Contreras the time of day.

Savanna's gushing over the bastard made him even more wary. If she was some sort of investigator, her behavior made sense. He still hadn't had a chance to check her ID. He was going to have to stay heads-up until Kurt was free. Hell would freeze over before he let Savanna and Contreras be alone together.

Ben resettled his hat low on his brow, leaned back in the seat, and smiled. Savanna might be as stubborn as a two-headed mule, but he'd decided that he wanted her—no matter what her game was. He'd been waiting around a long time for somebody like her to come along, and he'd be damned if he let her go without a fight. If he put his mind to it, he could be twice as stubborn as Savanna on her best day.

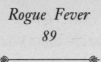

By noon Savanna was more than willing to take a break. She hadn't seen diddly-squat that looked like a landing strip. She hadn't seen an airplane or a hangar or even a wind sock. She *had* seen miles and miles of pasture and fences and black cows. She'd also seen the entrance to Don Luna's ranch house, but it had a gate and a couple of men working near it. She couldn't very well simply wheel in and declare that she was lost if she got stopped. Especially not with Ben along.

She pulled over on a deserted stretch. "This looks like a good place for lunch," she said, pointing to a spot in a pasture. "At least it has some trees for shade."

"It also has a fence."

"You can't climb a fence?"

"Hell, yeah, I can climb a fence, but it's trespassing."

She grinned. "Let's live dangerously." She got out and headed for the fence, leaving Ben to mutter something about "trouble" and bring up the rear with the cooler.

"Dammit, wait a minute."

When he caught up with her, he stepped on the bottom two strands of barbed wire and held up the top one, making a spot for her to climb between. He handed the cooler through the opening, then deftly slipped through himself.

They found a place where three large trees formed a shaded canopy, and Ben spread out a large red tablecloth on the ground.

"Very nice," she commented when she noticed the cloth and matching red napkins.

"Thanks." He handed her a bottle of orange juice, then set out tin plates, thick roast beef sandwiches, and melon slices. "I just hope I don't end up with a load of buckshot in my butt. It would be just my luck."

Savanna laughed, swigged the bottle of orange juice, then opened another and sat down on the cloth to drink it more leisurely while she enjoyed her sandwich.

Ben tossed his hat aside, ran his fingers through his damp hair, then sat down cross-legged beside her to eat.

When she finished, she stretched out her legs, leaned back on her elbows, and held her face up to the breeze. "It's very pleasant here, isn't it?"

"Mmmm."

"For a little of nothing, I could take a nap."

"All right by me." He patted his thigh. "You can use my lap as a pillow." She hesitated. "Come on. I promise I won't bite."

Still she hesitated.

"Chick-en," he teased softly.

She ground her teeth and settled her head in his lap. "If I drop off, don't let me sleep more than ten minutes. Promise?"

"I promise."

Ten minutes later Ben was looking down at the unguarded face, so sweet, so innocent, so lovely in sleep. He wanted to kiss her. Badly. But he didn't. He carefully brushed a wisp of hair from her cheek and curled it around his finger. His thumb rubbed the blond strand. Soft. Silky.

He'd watched Savanna from the moment her eyes had closed, a poignant ache squeezing at his heart the whole time. The more he'd watched her, the more he was sure that this was the woman for him. With Kurt's business to be taken care of, he wasn't sure how he'd work out the logistics, but he would.

Funny how quickly it had happened. Almost from the minute she'd walked into the cantina, he'd known. Something had socked him in the gut and said, "This is it." He'd ignored the feeling at first, pushed it aside and concentrated on the lust that had come along with it. The feeling had become too strong to ignore. Like a pair of powerful magnets straining toward each other. Magnetism. That was it. He wondered if she felt it too.

He hated to wake her, but he'd promised.

He plucked a seed head from a clump of grass and brushed it across her nose.

She swatted at it, turned on her side, and curled her arm around his thigh. Her hand was tucked near a very sensitive place.

He stiffened. In more ways than one.

"Savanna." He shook her shoulder.

She came awake, sat up, and stretched. "Has it been ten minutes already?"

"More like fifteen. You want to sleep some more?"

"No. We'd better get on the road." She stood and grabbed that monster of a purse she always carried and looped the strap over her head and under one arm.

They'd started replacing their stuff in the cooler, when Ben heard a familiar noise—a low snort. His hands froze around the tablecloth he'd picked up to fold. His blood ran cold.

He glanced up to see a giant of a bull about fifty yards away. Bred for his fighting spirit with horns like lances and shoulders like a brick wall, the black devil was eyeing them with territorial fury.

"Oh, hell."

"What's the matter?" Savanna asked, about to turn.

"Don't move," Ben commanded softly. "Don't move a muscle."

"Why not?"

She whirled around, and the bull snorted, lowered his head, and pawed the ground.

"Oh, hell," she whispered, echoing his comment.

The bull snorted and pawed the ground again.

"When I say run, you run like the devil and jump the fence," Ben said.

"It's too far. We'll never make it."

"I'll distract him with this tablecloth."

"You run. *I'll* distract him." She grabbed for the red cloth.

"Dammit, woman! You're the most stubborn—"

The bull snorted again and charged.

As the Mexican fighting bull thundered toward them, Ben cursed and shoved Savanna toward the nearest tree. "Climb," he shouted, boosting her bottom.

"Ha! *Toro!*" Ben held out the red tablecloth and flapped it, hoping to buy her time to scale the tree.

True to his breeding, the big black demon lowered his head and charged the moving object. At the last moment Ben released his makeshift cape so that it caught on the bull's horns and covered his face. While the bull snorted and tossed his head to shake off the tablecloth, Ben scrambled up the same tree Savanna had climbed.

Ben didn't stop until he was well clear of

the ground, legs spread with one foot on one branch, the other foot on a second one, and his arms wrapped around the trunk. And talk about sweating. He was wringing wet.

He heard a giggle over his head and looked up to see Savanna sitting in the tree fork a couple of feet above. She shouted, "*¡Ole!*" and clapped her hands. "If I had a rose, I'd throw it."

"It isn't funny, Savanna. That son of a bitch could have killed us."

"But he didn't. Great cape work. Why did you stop?"

Ben climbed up closer to her. "Because I'm not a fool. Have you ever seen somebody after they've been gored?"

"Can't say that I have."

"It's not pretty." He straddled a sturdy limb and held on to one fork of the trunk where she sat. "Why didn't you run when I told you to?"

"What? And let you have all the fun alone?"

He scowled. "You thought that was fun?"

"Now that it's over and nobody got hurt, yeah, I did. It was exciting. Tell me the truth, didn't you get a charge out of playing matador? You were really grand."

His scowl gradually faded. "You thought I was grand?"

"Absolutely." She leaned over and kissed him briefly.

"For another one of those, I might be willing to climb down and have another go at *el toro*."

"Don't press your luck." She leaned over and peered down. "Uh-oh."

Ben looked to see what had prompted her comment. The bull was back, and he was trashing the cooler, snorting and butting it with his head. "Dammit, he's stomped my hat all to hell."

"Better your hat than your body."

"That's for sure."

"Uh, Ben?"

"Yeah?"

"How are we going to get down?"

"We'll have to wait until Ferdinand decides to leave."

Half an hour later Savanna asked, "Has he gone yet?"

Ben parted the leafy branches and peered through them. "Nope. He's standing about ten feet away. I think he's grinning at me."

"Want to play twenty questions some more?"

He shook his head. "I'd give a hundred dollars for a drink of water right now."

Savanna dragged her purse around to her

lap. "Put your money where your mouth is."
She unzipped the bag and pulled out a plastic
bottle.

An hour later Savanna shifted on her
perch. "I don't know about you, but my
fanny's going numb."

Ben chuckled. "You don't happen to have a
couple of cushions in that purse of yours, do
you?"

She opened the bag and playfully peeked
inside. "Nope, no cushions. But I have a miniature chess set. Want to play?"

"I don't know how."

She sighed. "Me neither or I'd teach you."

"Why do you carry a chess set if you don't
know how to play?"

"It came in the package with the miniature
cribbage board."

"I can play cribbage."

"So can I, but I lost the board. I still have
the deck of cards. Want to play some gin
rummy?"

He shrugged. "Why not? It looks like
we're going to be up here for a while. With my
luck I should have known better than to cross
that fence."

"What does luck have to do with it?" she
asked as she patted her purse to make a playing
surface.

"Anytime I stray from the straight and narrow, I get in trouble." He told her about a dozen things that had happened when he was a kid. "When I was a senior in high school, a bunch of guys decided to paint the water tower in town. We saw the police coming, scrambled down in a hurry, and took off running. Everybody got away except me. I stepped in a gopher hole and sprained my ankle. Besides having to be out for most of basketball season, I caught holy hell at home."

"From your father?"

"No. From my mother. She's a war horse. She made me write a letter of apology to the town and put it in the local newspaper. When my ankle healed, I had to scrub every drop of spray paint off the water tower. It was a bitch." He chuckled. "Not that it did much good. Another bunch of kids sprayed it the next week. But *I* didn't join them. I never painted another water tower, but I got in trouble a few times in college. Poor Kurt is just like me."

Savanna shuffled the cards and dealt. "Who is Kurt?"

"My nephew. My oldest sister Ellen's son. He's the reason I'm down here. He's in jail."

"In *jail*? Where?"

"In Tres Lunas."

"I didn't know they had a jail."

"Yep. And he's been in it for over two

weeks. Makes me madder than the devil to think about it."

"What in the world did he do?" she asked, discarding the three of clubs.

Ben picked up the three. "He had a little fender-bender."

"And he's in *jail* for having a car accident?"

"It's complicated. He and two of his buddies decided to take a trip to Mexico when their final exams were over. So they all piled into Kurt's pickup, a new Ford extended cab, and took off. They knocked around here and there and ended up in Tres Lunas. To make a long story short, Kurt ran into the rear fender of an old Chevy that came barreling out of a side street. Unfortunately, the old Chevy belonged to the *delegado*. He's sort of the Mexican equivalent to a sheriff or a village police chief. Even more unfortunately, Kurt hadn't thought to buy Mexican automobile insurance."

"Uh-oh," Savanna said. "I know what sticklers they are for that."

"You got it. The other two boys hopped a bus home, but Kurt's truck was confiscated, and he was sentenced to six months in jail."

"*Six* months?"

"Yep. Gin." He spread his winning hand on her purse.

"But that's ridiculous."

"Sure it's ridiculous, but that's the way it

is. Kurt didn't realize how serious his situation was, and his parents didn't know about it until he'd been sentenced. Ellen is a basket case over it. Since I'm the only one in the family who speaks Spanish, I came down to try to buy him out."

"Buy him out?"

"To grease a few palms and get Kurt and his truck back. But it seems that Delegado Ortiz and his family are on vacation in his new Ford pickup. Hell, the bastard can keep the truck, but I want Kurt released."

"Do you think you can get him out?"

Ben's jaw tightened. "I'm going to. One way or another."

He wasn't a crook or a lawman after all. Savanna gave a small sigh of relief.

"What's that about?"

"I was just thinking about something. You really are a rancher, aren't you?"

"Of course. Are you really a botanist?"

"Why else would I be here?"

He cocked one eyebrow and said, "Indeed. Why else would you be here?"

Two hours later Savanna licked chocolate from her fingers. "Sure you don't want a Snickers?"

"No thanks." He shifted his position in the tree. "I wish we hadn't lost those cards."

"Me too."

An errant gust of wind had carried away six cards from the discard pile before they could catch them. Five ended on the ground. The queen of hearts was caught in a tree limb too far away to reach.

"Where's Ferdinand?" Savanna asked.

Ben parted the branches. "Still in sight. Too close to chance it." He shifted position again so that his back was against the trunk and away from Savanna. After a long period of silence, he said, "I've told you my entire life story since we've been up here, and you haven't told me anything about yourself. I know about your parents, but tell me about your aunt and uncle."

"I'd rather not discuss them."

"Okay."

They sat quietly for a long time. Memories of her childhood, awful memories, crept into her consciousness. Some strange compulsion made her want to tell Ben about them. She ignored the feeling. She hadn't discussed that part of her life with anyone since she was fourteen.

"My aunt and uncle lived on a turkey farm," she said softly.

"A turkey farm?"

"Yes. I was a city girl; I hated it. And I hated them and their odious brat of a son Eddie."

She didn't say any more for a while, and Ben didn't push. They simply sat in the tree and listened to the rustle of leaves and the chirr of grasshoppers in the field.

She sighed and swallowed the lump that knotted in her throat. "I was eight when I went to live with them; Eddie was ten. My job was to feed the chickens and gather eggs from the henhouse. It was dark in that henhouse, and it smelled. Eddie told me that there were rats and snakes and crawly bugs and sharp-toothed monsters in the henhouse, and I grew terrified of going in there."

"That little snot! Didn't you tell your aunt and uncle?"

"I told them. I wept and begged not to have to gather the eggs. They told me that was nonsense and made me do it anyway. If I balked, Aunt Emma would slap me or Uncle Sid would whip me with his belt." Once started, Savanna couldn't stop the words from tumbling out. She told him of her uncle's drinking and the beatings she'd endured. She told him of dragging her dresser across the door every night to keep her uncle—and later her cousin—from coming in her room at night.

Ben swore softly. "God, Savanna, I hate that you had to endure that. Why didn't you tell somebody? A teacher? A minister? Somebody."

"I did try to talk to our preacher about the beatings when I was about eleven. My aunt and uncle attended a hellfire and brimstone fundamentalist church. The preacher gave me a lecture about sparing the rod and spoiling the child, then told my uncle about my talking to him. My back bled through my nightgown that night. I was too terrified to talk to anyone after that."

"Dammit!"

"When I was fourteen, Eddie, who was a big, strapping sixteen-year-old, cornered me in the henhouse one evening. When he started to tear my clothes off, I kneed him in the groin, hit him with the egg bucket, and knocked him cold. I ran and barricaded myself in my room. The next day at school I went to the counselor's office first thing. I never saw my aunt and uncle or Eddie again."

"May they rot in hell."

"May they rot in hell," she repeated.

"And after that?"

"After that I went to live with Don and Nancy Malmquist, the sweetest couple on the face of the earth. They gave me back my dignity."

"And you've lived happily ever after?"

She laughed. "For the most part. And now I don't take any bull from anybody." Craning her neck, she scanned the pasture. "Speaking of bull, where's ours?"

"He meandered off over that rise while you were talking. I think he's gone—at least for a while. Let's light a shuck before he decides to come back. Let me go first."

Ben climbed down and helped Savanna. They quickly gathered the trashed remnants of their picnic and, stiff-legged, made their way back to the Jeep.

"Have you had about enough for one day?" Ben asked.

"Yep. I want to soak my fanny for at least an hour."

He hugged her to him and kissed her cheek. "You can have the bathroom first. Put on some of that good-smelling perfume. I've planned a special dinner for us tonight."

SIX

"Ah, Señor Favor. *¡Buenas noches!*" Pepe said as he held open the door to the jail.

Ben carried the dinner tray inside and asked in Spanish, "How's Kurt this evening? Maria said that he wasn't feeling well earlier."

"No bueno," Pepe said, frowning and rubbing his ample stomach to indicate the source of Kurt's distress.

"Would you let me have five minutes with him?"

"Ah, Señor Favor, alas, I cannot do that. No visitors without Delegado Ortiz's permission, and he is still on vacation. But he will be back tomorrow."

"I've heard that before."

"No, no, it is true. He telephoned an hour ago. He will be in his office at nine o'clock tomorrow morning."

Ben balanced the tray with one hand and pulled out a new hundred-peso note. He put it on the desk and said, "I would be deeply grateful for two minutes with Kurt. His mother is very concerned about his health."

"Ah, for his mother. Very well. Two minutes. No more." Pepe took a ring of keys from a wall hook. "Follow me."

Breathing a soft sigh of relief, Ben followed the jailer after he unlocked a door and led him back to the cell area. He'd been able to bribe his way in to seeing Kurt only a few times since he'd been in Tres Lunas.

Ben was shocked at what he found—not at the condition of the cell, which was primitive by U.S. standards, but by Kurt's appearance. He looked as if he'd lost ten pounds in the few days since he'd seen him. Hollow-eyed and pale, Kurt lay listlessly on the cot.

"Hey, pardner," Ben said. "How's it going?"

Kurt sat up slowly, then rose and came to the bars. "Not good, Ben. Not good. Montezuma's revenge, I guess. I hope you can get me out of this hellhole soon."

"Just hang on for a day or two longer. The *delegado* is coming back tomorrow. We'll work something out. I brought you your dinner."

"I can't eat it. I haven't been able to handle anything but liquids for a couple of days."

"Why in the hell didn't somebody tell me? Who's been eating the meals I send?"

Kurt shrugged and glanced at Pepe.

Ben suspected that Pepe understood more English than he let on. When Ben turned to glare at him, he looked guilty as sin. "Kurt is very sick, Pepe. He needs a doctor."

"Tres Lunas is a small village. We have no doctor. Your time is up. Come."

"Kurt, I'll try to get you some medicine. Just hang on, buddy. Hang on."

Ben muttered curses all the way back to the hotel, the dull expression in Kurt's eyes dogging his steps. He only hoped that swaggering sleazeball Ricardo would come through for him. He'd promised Contreras ten thousand dollars to pay off the police, get Kurt released, and fly them home. Contreras had sworn that it would be no problem, but he was beginning to worry if Don Luna's son-in-law had the clout to carry it off. Although out of respect for the don nobody said much about Contreras, it was obvious that he wasn't highly regarded in Tres Lunas.

Savanna stood on tiptoe, trying to see as much of herself as she could in the old dresser mirror. She smiled. Very nice, if she did say so herself.

Ben had said that he'd planned a special

dinner, and she hated to wear shorts or jeans for the occasion. So while he was in the shower, she'd hurried down to the shop on the plaza. The blue embroidered dress had fit her perfectly.

Now she was in her new dress with her hair down and makeup on, waiting for Ben's knock. She added another touch of Safari between her breasts and dropped the sample bottle into her cavernous bag. If everything went as planned the next day, this would be her last night in Tres Lunas, the last night she would have with Ben. And she meant to enjoy herself.

In the short time since she'd been there, they'd spent a lot of hours together, and her attraction to him hadn't abated one iota. In truth, it had grown enormously, especially after their encounter with Ferdinand. A powerful bonding had occurred between them while they were stuck in that tree. After their intimate conversation and his sensitive response to her past, she felt very close to him.

Very close.

And now she felt very . . . romantic.

And very, very sexy.

Laughing, she twirled around, and her full skirt billowed out. And if one thing led to another, then why not? She was an adult.

Not that she intended to jump his bones and take him to bed, of course. It was just that if one thing *did* lead to another, she wouldn't complain too loudly.

What a difference a day made.

She was still giddy and smiling when a knock came at the door and she opened it. Her smile died when she saw Ben's expression. "Ben, what's wrong?"

He raked his fingers through his hair. "Kurt's in a mess. He's sick, and there isn't a doctor in this town." He related the details of his visit with his nephew. "I'm worried about him, Savanna. Really worried."

"Stop worrying. We're going to do something about it. Go downstairs and see if Maria has any chicken"—she shuddered—"or beef broth. No spices, only salt. Also get plenty of Pepsi and mineral water. I have some stuff that I think will help. And get some fresh bed linens while you're at it. You don't happen to have an extra pair of pajamas, do you?"

"I don't sleep in pajamas."

"Oh. No matter. Does Kurt have clean clothes?"

"Should have. I've paid Pepe's wife to wash them."

"Good. Well, don't just stand there with your mouth open, Ben. Get going. I'll meet you at the desk."

He saluted. "Yes, ma'am."

After he left, Savanna dug through the contents of her duffel and her shoulder bag.

She set out a plastic grocery sack, a small box of saltine crackers, a quart of Gatorade, a hotel-size bar of soap, a thermometer, and four vials of pills. She dumped everything into the grocery sack, then threw in a can of disinfectant and the paperback she'd been reading for good measure and went downstairs.

Ben was waiting with a small container of iced drinks in his hands and a stack of linens under his arm. "Maria had some broth at home. She's gone to get it. What do you have there?" he asked.

"Crackers, Gatorade, Lomotil for if he has Montezuma's revenge, antibiotics if it's something else, aspirin, and vitamin C. Plus a couple of other things."

As soon as Maria returned with the broth, Savanna and Ben set off across the plaza toward the jail.

"I just hope Pepe will let us in to see Kurt."

"I think he will. Let me handle it. Does he speak English?"

"Not much."

"Then you translate."

Pepe opened the door when Ben knocked. "Ah, Señor Favor." Seeing Savanna, he grinned lasciviously and ogled her bosom.

Dear Lord, he was the man who'd seen her when she'd leaned out the window to watch the plane. She cleared her throat and he looked up sheepishly. Head high, she walked briskly into the office with the two men following her. She noticed a half-eaten tray of food on the desk and a ragged copy of *Penthouse* opened and lying facedown beside it.

She lifted her chin, turned to the jailer, and said with all the authority she could muster, "Señor, I am a gold star nurse with the Peace Corps's World Health Association. I am charged with seeing to the health of individuals incarcerated in countries outside their natural domicile. I have come to treat your prisoner." She turned to Ben. "Translate."

Ben made a choking sound, covered it with a cough, then spoke to Pepe in Spanish. Pepe looked puzzled, then replied in Spanish.

"He says you'll need his boss's permission first."

"Tell him that I have authority from the United Nations. This could cause an international incident."

Ben translated. Pepe scratched his head and looked pained.

"Tell him that if he doesn't let me in, I'll tell his wife what he's been reading." She jerked her head toward the magazine.

Ben choked and coughed again, then translated. Pepe looked even more pained.

"Take us to the prisoner," Savanna demanded.

"*Sí*, señorita." He quickly unlocked and opened the door.

Savanna brushed past him and strode down the dim corridor as if she owned the place. She stopped at the cell where Kurt lay curled on a cot. "Unlock it!"

Pepe hesitated only a second. "*Sí*, señorita."

She looked around and wrinkled her nose. "This place is a pigsty. It must be swept and mopped." She pointed to the toilet and the sink. "Filthy. Scrub it!"

Ben translated. Pepe said, "*Sí*, señorita," and hopped to it.

Kurt had roused and was watching the activity, frowning. "Ben? What's going on? How did you get in here?"

"Don't ask." Ben laughed. "Meet Savanna Smith, a friend of mine. She's a combination Carrie Nation, Florence Nightingale, and drill sergeant. She's brought you some medicine."

Savanna grinned at the dark-haired boy who looked like a younger, slimmer version of his uncle. "Hi, Kurt. Feeling pretty punk, huh."

"Yeah. Lousy."

She felt his forehead. "I don't think you have fever, but let's check." She stuck the thermometer under his tongue and took his pulse. Or, rather, for Pepe's benefit she acted as if she were taking his pulse. The jailer had stopped his sweeping to watch her. She glared at him, and the broom started moving vigorously.

"Nope," she said a couple of minutes later. "No fever." She shook out a pair of tiny white tablets for Kurt. "Take two of these now, then one every six hours until you're better. And take one of these antibiotics every four hours just to be on the safe side." She gave him another pill and opened the Gatorade to wash them down. "Now take a vitamin C for me. I'm convinced that it cures everything." She smiled and winked.

His bed was nothing but an old army cot with a thin mattress, a stained pillow, and a ratty, scratchy blanket. Savanna said, "While your uncle helps you wash up and put on a fresh T-shirt, I'm going to make your bed."

She shook out everything and sprayed it with Lysol, then hummed as she smoothed clean linens on the lumpy mattress. When Ben helped him back to bed, she asked Kurt, "Does that feel better?"

"Yes, it does. Now, if my stomach would only behave—"

"It's going to be fine. Lord, I've had the wretched stuff. For a while you feel like you're going to die, but it gets better. You need to sip a little broth and eat a cracker now and then. Drink the rest of the Gatorade and as many liquids as you can tolerate. Don't drink any water unless it's bottled mineral water."

"Thanks, Savanna," Kurt said.

"No problem." She smiled and touched his cheek. "Rest now if you can. I'll check on you in the morning." She glanced at Pepe, who was industriously scouring the sink. The cell wouldn't win any housekeeping awards, but it was considerably cleaner than when they'd arrived.

"Señor," she said, addressing the jailer. "I'm leaving some medicine for Kurt to take. Be sure and remind him in four hours and six hours."

After translating, Ben said, "Pepe goes off duty at two A.M. His cousin Jesus comes on then."

"Then have him tell Jesus what to do. We'll be back early in the morning to examine Kurt again."

When they were ready to leave, she inspected the sink. It was stained and chipped but reasonably clean. "*Bueno*, señor. *Muchas gracias.*"

Pepe beamed as if she'd pinned a medal on him.

They left the jail quickly and had barely made it out the front door, when Ben's shoulders began shaking with stifled laughter. "A gold star nurse? The Peace Corps's World Health Association?"

She grinned. "So I made it up. It got us in, didn't it?"

He hugged her against his side as they walked. "Lord, woman, you're a treasure."

"I'm also hungry."

"One candlelight dinner coming up."

They sat beneath a latticed arch in the small courtyard behind the hotel, votive candles flickering on the table and luminarias glowing around the base of the wall. Jose sat unobtrusively in a shadowy corner, strumming soft, sweet tunes, just as Ben had paid him to do. Juan's mother had provided the roses for the table, and their scents, along with the piquant spices from their meal, wafted through the balmy evening air.

Juan and Maria had done a good job with the spot and with the meal. They'd thought the idea was beautifully romantic. It was a start. When they got back to the States and things got untangled, Ben planned to court Savanna in style. After the life she'd lived, she deserved nothing but the best—and he meant to give it to her. Hearing about the abuse she'd endured as a child had cut him to the quick. And though he was no psychologist, he understood why she'd armored herself with a sassy manner and an independent streak.

She was some kind of woman. He admired her.

And he wanted her.

The rising moon, almost full, shone through the open lattice above and turned Savanna's hair to glistening silver. He ached to reach out and touch it, but he didn't. If he'd had any doubts that he was falling for her in a big way, her actions at the jail would have erased them. She'd charged in like an avenging angel and turned Pepe to mush. The tender way she'd treated Kurt had turned Ben to mush. She would make a wonderful mother.

He smiled. "Have I told you how lovely you look tonight?"

"No, I don't believe that you have." She sipped apple juice from a wineglass.

"Well, you do." He plucked a red rose from the vase on the table, touched her cheek with the full blossom, then offered it to her.

"Thank you." She held the rose to her nose and breathed in its fragrance.

"Are you ready for coffee and dessert?"

"Anytime."

"I'll tell Juan."

Savanna watched him disappear inside, then closed her eyes and let the soft music and warm scents wash over her. This was the most romantic evening she'd ever spent with a man. Funny, she'd never pegged Ben Favor as a romantic. Obviously he was, since he'd arranged all this. But then, she'd never considered herself romantic either. Ben was bringing out all sorts of things in her.

She thought of what was to come later, and her lips tingled with the memory of his mouth on hers. Desire swelled inside her, making her shiver.

Warm lips brushed her forehead. She opened her eyes.

"You look a million miles away," Ben said as he sat down.

She smiled. "No, not that far." *Only as far as my bedroom.*

Juan entered with a tray. He served coffee, then was about to pour a cruet of something onto what looked like a molded flan.

"Let me," Ben said, taking the cruet. He winked at Savanna, upended the bottle, saturating the dessert, and held a match to a votive candle flame until it flared.

"Señor Ben!"

Ben held the match to the flan. Flames shot six feet into the air.

Savanna yelped.

Jose hit a sour note.

Juan shouted in Spanish.

Ben cursed in English.

And the wooden lattice, tinder dry, caught on fire.

Luckily, a bucket of mop water was handy. Ben stood on a chair and splashed it on the burning lattice, and the fire fizzled into curling wisps of smoke.

The flan didn't fare well.

Both Ben and the table were dripping with dirty water. Juan stood to one side, wringing his hands and muttering. Jose and his guitar disappeared.

Looking thoroughly disgusted with himself, Ben said, "God, Savanna, I'm sorry about this mess. Are you okay?"

"Well, my bangs are a little singed, but otherwise I'm fine."

Obviously alarmed, he stared at her forehead. "You don't have bangs."

"Must have been singed worse than I thought."

"It's not funny."

"Oh, Señor Ben, I'm so sorry," Juan said, looking totally miserable. "You poured too much liqueur on the flan. It takes only *un poco*." He measured a small amount with his fingers.

He scowled. "Now you tell me."

Savanna tried to keep a straight face, but she couldn't. Between gales of laughter she said, "Yes, it is funny."

Hands on his hips, Ben surveyed the charred wood overhead and the dripping mess on the table and continued to scowl.

Savanna made a *V* with her index and middle fingers and pushed the corners of his mouth upward. "Smile," she said. "Don't be such an ogre. You're scaring Juan to death. Think of this as an adventure."

The forced smile turned into a chuckle. "It is kind of funny, isn't it?"

She nodded.

Ben put his arm around her waist and said, "Juan, my apologies for all this." He gestured toward the destruction. "I'll pay for getting everything fixed." Juan tried to argue graciously, but Ben held firm. To Savanna he said, "Let's get out of here. The place smells terrible, and I'm wet. Did I get any water on you?"

"Not a drop."

"I want to run upstairs and take a quick shower and change clothes. Have a cup of coffee in the cantina, and I'll be right back." His boots took the steps two at a time.

Before she'd finished her coffee, Ben was back, his hair still damp. "Want to go for a walk?" he asked.

Holding hands, they made two turns around the plaza, then sat down on the rim of the fountain and looked at the moon.

"I wish there was something more exciting to do around here," Ben said. "This must be a pretty dull date for you."

"Is this a date?"

"You betcha." He smiled. "When are you going back to Dallas?"

"In another day or two. What about you? When are you going back to Alvin?"

He shrugged. "Depends on when I can get Kurt released. Soon, I hope." He lifted her hand to his lips and brushed his lips against it.

That simple act brought tears to her eyes, and she never cried. Her chest felt tight, achy. The thought of never seeing Ben again grew overwhelming.

But they had tonight. At least she would have a lovely memory.

She tugged at his hand. "Let's go in."

Arms around each other's waists, they walked slowly to the hotel and upstairs.

Savanna unlocked her door and turned to him, waiting for him to make the next move. His hand cupped her cheek, and his eyes scanned her face with such tenderness that her heart wrenched.

"You are so beautiful," he murmured, his mouth lowering a fraction of an inch toward hers. "You are so . . ."

Almost breathless, she waited for his next word. Sexy? Desirable?

". . . so sweet."

"*Sweet?* Me?"

"Yes, you." He kissed her then, a long, lingering, soul-stealing kiss.

She returned it with a lifetime of pent-up passion.

When his mouth left hers, she sighed, and

eyes closed, waited for him to sweep her into his brawny arms and carry her into the bedroom.

He dropped a peck on her nose and said, "Good night, darlin'."

Savanna's eyes popped open. He was walking toward the stairs.

"Ben Favor! Where are you going?"

"I thought I'd go downstairs and have a beer."

"A *beer*?"

"Yep."

She stuck her fists on her hips. "Well, you just go have a beer. Have two. Have a whole case, dammit!"

She stomped inside and slammed the door.

*G*et a *F*riend to join, and...
*G*et a *F*REE *N*ecklace and *P*endant!

See details below.   Detach and Mail Now!

For You: Get a FREE Necklace and Pendant

12732

❏ **YES!** My friend wants to be a Loveswept subscriber. Send me my FREE Necklace and Pendant as soon as my friend accepts her/his introductory shipment.

Name

Address

City   State   Zip

Membership #

For Your Friend: A FREE Mystery Gift plus 4 *Loveswept* Romances at Over 50% Off!

❏ **YES!** Send me my introductory shipment of 4 Loveswept Romances for a 15-day risk-free examination. If I keep the books I will pay only $4.98 (plus shipping and handling, and sales tax in NY, and GST in Canada) — **over 50% off** the low regular price, currently just $2.66 per book.* Then, about once a month, I will receive 4 new books hot off the presses, *before they're in the bookstores*, and from time to time, special editions of select Loveswept Romances at the low regular price, on a fully-refundable 15-day, risk-free trial basis. There is no minimum number of books to buy. I may return unwanted shipments at your expense, and cancel my subscription at any time.

Also, please send me my free Mystery Gift, mine to keep no matter what I decide.

4M108   70300

Name

Address

City   State   Zip

Telephone

Signature

DETACH CAREFULLY AND MAIL NOW!

Send No Money! No Obligation to Buy! Act Now!

*Plus shipping and handling, and sales tax in NY, and GST in Canada. Prices slightly higher in Canada. Prices subject to change. Orders subject to approval.

Get a Friend to join, then...
Get a FREE Necklace and Pendant!
Your Friend Gets 4 *Loveswept* Romances
at Over 50% Off...Plus a FREE Mystery Gift!

Turn over for details.

SEVEN

Bleary-eyed, Savanna wandered into the cantina the following morning and said to Juan, "Coffee, please. A gallon."

"A gallon?"

"I'll start with one cup. Maybe that will get me moving."

Juan chuckled. "Oh, you made a joke. You want breakfast now?"

"Coffee first. Then I'll think about it." She joined Ben, who was eating at their usual table.

"Good morning," he said.

"That's a matter of opinion." She glanced at the runny eggs on his plate and shuddered when he shoveled some in his mouth. "I don't know how you can eat that."

"I like eggs. Over easy with lots of black pepper."

Juan brought coffee, and she concentrated

on it while Ben finished the meal he seemed to relish.

When he was done, she found him studying her. "You're not really allergic to eggs, are you?"

"It depends on how you define *allergic*."

"Hives, stomachaches, nausea, something like that."

"Then I'm allergic. I try to eat eggs, I barf. Hadn't we better go check on Kurt?"

"I was at the jail half an hour ago. He's much better. He said to tell you thanks, and that you're a lifesaver. Have eggs always made you barf?"

"No, only since a year or two after I went to live with my aunt and uncle. I know what you're getting at, and I'm not interested in a therapy session. I don't eat eggs; I don't eat chicken; I don't eat turkey; I don't eat anything with feathers. Period. End of discussion."

"Testy this morning, aren't we? Didn't you sleep well?"

"I slept fine." *Liar*.

She saw amusement play at the corners of his mouth. "I didn't sleep worth a damn," he said. "I was too hot."

Oh, Lord, so was I, Savanna thought. But the room temperature wasn't a factor. She wondered if he'd had the same problem. She hoped he had. It was good enough for him. The rogue.

"You ready for breakfast now?" When she nodded, he motioned to Juan. "Are we going out looking for plants again this morning?"

"No. Ricardo's coming by to take me for a plane ride, remember?"

"Oh, yes. Ricardo. How could I forget?"

A muscle jumped in his jaw, and Savanna almost laughed aloud. He *was* jealous. The idea pleased her enormously, and her spirits lifted considerably.

After she'd eaten, she said, "I'm going up to my room and freshen up, maybe put on some lipstick."

Ben's eyes went cold. "For that pipsqueak with a ponytail?"

"No. For me. Why don't you stay here and have a *beer*?"

"Hold it." He grabbed her arm as she started to rise. "Is that what you're on your high horse about?"

"My high horse? I don't know what you're talking about."

"Last night when I said I was going downstairs to have a beer, you slammed your door hard enough to crack the plaster. Savanna, I'm no alcoholic. I've knocked back a lot of Carta Blanca since I've been in Tres Lunas, but at home I drink a beer or have a social drink only now and then. Does that bother you?"

"I've told you that it's your life and your liver."

"Then what made you mad? Except for the fire, I thought things went great last night."

Savanna felt like such an idiot. She wasn't about to tell him what her problem had been. "Last night was wonderful, Ben. Just chalk up my behavior to one of those women things."

"Ohhh," he said.

"Excuse me." She hurried up to her room, feeling like a traitor to womanhood for lying and using that excuse. But she'd learned to use any edge she could to hold her own and compete in what was still a man's world—particularly in her line of work. Which was why she didn't feel a bit guilty about putting on paint and powder and perfume in anticipation of Ricardo's arrival.

Macho chiseling jerk that he was, he'd never suspect that she was about to repossess his plane.

Ben was waiting outside when the red Corvette drove up and stopped. He walked over. "Ricardo. *¿Como esta?* I hope you had a good trip."

"Muy bien. Gracias." The little bastard gave him a perfunctory smile and looked around. "Where is Miss Smith? I've come to pick her up for a ride in my plane."

"She'll be down in a minute. Delegado Ortiz is back in town. I saw Kurt's truck in front of his house."

"I'll speak with him later."

"Speak with him now. Kurt is sick, and I'd like to get him back home as soon as possible."

"You have the money? In American dollars?"

"It's in Juan's safe. As soon as Kurt's free, I'll give you half. When we land at Clover Field, I'll give you the other half."

"I'll be back shortly," Contreras said. He got in his car and slung dust until he turned the corner.

Ortiz lived at the edge of town by the river, only a short distance away. Earlier that morning Ben had walked it in five minutes.

He leaned against a post and waited in front of the hotel. In about fifteen minutes Ricardo's Corvette roared to a stop, and he got out.

"Everything go okay?" Ben asked.

"A small problem."

Ben went on alert, but he kept his bearing casual. "A problem?"

"Delegado Ortiz is willing to convert your nephew's jail sentence to a fine, but the price will be twenty thousand dollars. American."

"*¡Hijo de puta!*" Ben cursed. "You said ten. I don't have twenty thousand dollars." That was a lie; he'd brought more than that with him, but he wasn't about to let this sorry low-life know it.

Ricardo shrugged. "What can I say? Ortiz is a greedy man. I tried to argue with him, but he was firm."

Ben was over a barrel. He knew he could probably bargain them down in a few days, but he wanted to get Kurt home quickly. To hell with it. "Okay. When can we leave? The sooner, the better. I'm ready now."

Ricardo grinned. "So you do have twenty thousand with you?"

Uh-oh. Thinking fast, he said, "No, I'll have to borrow the rest from my friend."

"Miss Smith?" His grin widened. "She is a wealthy woman?"

"Keep your hands off her, Contreras. She's mine."

"But I think she likes me."

"Forget it. When can we leave?"

"Not until early tomorrow morning. There are arrangements to be made, papers to fill out, that sort of thing. Ah, Miss Smith. *¡Buenos días!*"

Ben looked around to see Savanna coming toward them, hips swinging, a huge smile plastered on her face, and wearing makeup an inch thick. Her shirt was unbuttoned almost to her navel, and he could swear that those white shorts were shorter. That feed bag of a purse was slung over her shoulder and made her

shirt gap open so that a good expanse of cleavage showed. He'd bet that Contreras's eyes
were bugged out of his head. He knew his
were.

"*¡Buenos días!*" she said, holding out her
hand to Ricardo. He brought it to his lips. She
gave his hand a squeeze and smiled brightly.
"I've so been looking forward to flying in your
plane. And your Corvette is *beautiful.*" She
lightly ran her fingers over the fender and fluttered her eyelashes.

Ben thought he was going to puke.

"Then shall we go?" Ricardo gallantly
opened the door on the passenger side.

Before she could move, Ben deftly slid into
the seat.

"What are you doing?" Savanna asked.

"I thought I'd go with you."

"But, Ben, the car has only two seats."

He shrugged. "You can sit in my lap."

She rolled her eyes, then glanced at Contreras. He shrugged.

She and her purse climbed in. She wiggled
a dozen times, poking and gouging as she settled in his lap and got her purse situated. He
could swear that she deliberately tried to maul
the family jewels, but he bit his tongue. If she
thought he was going to let her go off with
that pint-size Casanova by herself, she had another think coming.

Even though he'd rather be staked over an

anthill than zoom up in that plane, he was going. He still didn't know what Savanna was up to. And as crazy as he was about her, he didn't trust her motives. Until Kurt was safely home, he wasn't taking any chances. He might be crazy about her, but he wasn't crazy.

He put his arms around her waist to hold her still, then smiled and said, "Now, isn't this cozy?"

By the time they reached Don Luna's ranch, Savanna was considering murder. Ben had buttoned up her shirt to the very top, then stroked her leg and nuzzled her ear the entire trip. A fine time to get amorous!

She raked her heel down his shin and ground her bottom into his lap, but it didn't deter him. "Beennn," she squealed coyly, trying to trap his hand with hers as his thumb snaked beneath her shorts.

He only chuckled and nipped at her earlobe. She would have belted him, except that she didn't want to louse up the simpering-female act she was playing for Ricardo's benefit.

While she was trying to control Ben's hands and ignore his tongue in her ear—which wasn't easy—she carefully watched the route Ricardo took. He'd veered off to the left before he reached the complex of buildings where she assumed the main house was and drove down a dirt road for about a mile.

There it was! A hangar, an outbuilding, and a sweet blue and white Cessna 210 sitting at the edge of a landing strip.

Ricardo pulled up near the hangar and parked. When Ben opened the car door, she got out, making sure to step on his foot and clip him on the chin with her shoulder bag as she dragged it out behind her.

She scanned the area as she walked toward the plane. Not another soul stirred. Good. That would make her job easier.

"Oh, how lovely!" she gushed, clapping her hands and beaming at Ricardo.

He puffed up like a blowfish.

Ben limped toward them and gave the Cessna a once-over. "Not bad."

"Not bad?" Savanna said. "How can you say that? It's *beautiful*." It truly was a honey of a plane. She only wished she could afford it. She hadn't saved anywhere near the eighty or ninety thousand this baby would cost, but after another lucrative job like this one, she'd have enough for the smaller plane she'd had her eye on. She had to restrain herself from jumping in the cockpit and taking off at that very moment.

"Thank you, Miss Smith," Ricardo said. "This airplane is my greatest treasure."

"I would have thought your wife was," Ben muttered.

"Please call me Savanna," she said, ignoring Ben's comment. She walked to the passenger side of the Cessna. "How do we get in?"

Ricardo laughed and swaggered forward. He opened the door and pointed out the step. "This way."

"Oh . . . how . . . cute. Look, Ben, a little step built right in."

Ben made a gurgling noise and climbed into the plane.

"I want to sit in the front," she called after him.

"Okay by me." Ben took one of the back two seats.

What, no argument?

When everybody was strapped in, Savanna pointed to the gauges. "What are all the little thingies here?"

Ricardo explained each one to her.

"What makes it go?" she asked.

"The engine and the design of the plane."

"Does it use gasoline like a car?"

He smiled indulgently. "No, it requires a special fuel."

"Do you have to go to an airport to get it?"

"No, we have a tank here."

"Here? Where?"

Ricardo pointed to the fuel pump near the hangar.

"Well, if that isn't the neatest thing. You have your own filling station. I guess you have to keep it locked up to discourage thieves."

He laughed. "No. No locks here. No one would dare steal from Don Luna." He positioned the throttle, started the engine, and taxied down the runway.

She was grateful that he did a preflight check instead of hotdogging it. And his takeoff was smooth as silk. Soon they were cruising above Tres Lunas, then following the river with Ricardo pointing out areas of interest to her. She asked some more dumb questions so that he could show off by answering them.

"Oh, this is just so thrilling," she bubbled. "Isn't it thrilling, Ben? Ben?" She twisted around to look at him. He was ashen around the mouth, and his fingers gripped the seat arms in true white-knuckled fashion.

"Ben?" she asked again louder. "Are you okay?"

"I'm fine."

"You don't look fine. You look green around the gills."

"Must have been something I ate."

"Why didn't you say something? You could have stayed on the ground."

He gave her a *need-you-ask?* look. "Don't worry about me. I'm fine."

She touched Ricardo's arm. "I think we should go back now. Ben's not feeling well."

———◆———◆———

Ben was glad to get his feet planted back on terra firma. Strange that flying commercial jets didn't bother him, but flying in small planes bothered the hell out of him. Though he'd rather swallow a rattlesnake than admit it to Savanna.

Contreras drove them back to the hotel. He noticed that when Savanna got off his lap and out of the car, she didn't whack him with her purse again. Her Florence Nightingale persona, he supposed. Being kind to the sick and infirm.

"Ricardo, thank you so much," she said. "That was wonderful."

He bowed slightly. "My pleasure. Would you like to join me for dinner tonight at the ranch?"

"Will Señora Contreras be there?" she asked sweetly.

"Alas, no. She has gone with Don Luna to visit her aunt."

No way was she going out to that ranch. Ben put his arm around Savanna and hugged her possessively. "Sorry, Ricardo. We have other plans."

"Another time perhaps," she said.

"I shall look forward to it. *¡Adiós!*"

"Wait up a minute, Ricardo," Ben said. "I want to talk to you." He drew Savanna aside and said, "Would you excuse us for a minute, darlin'?"

She looked puzzled, then shrugged. "Sure. What plans do we have for tonight?"

"I thought we might replay our dinner from last night. But without the fire. Okay?"

She hesitated a moment, then said, "Okay."

"You want to go out looking at plants after lunch?"

"No, I think I'll spend the afternoon shopping."

"Shopping? In Tres Lunas? That should take about five minutes."

"You might be surprised." She smiled and gushed her thanks again to Ricardo, then went inside the hotel.

"What time are we going to leave in the morning?" Ben asked Contreras.

Ricardo thought for a minute. "I would like to leave at first light so that I will be able to return before dark. The airstrip is not equipped with lights. Shall we meet in front of the hotel at four-thirty?"

"Four-thirty? Isn't that a strange time of day to release Kurt?"

Contreras shrugged. "I will make the arrangements. After he is released, we will drive in my car directly to the plane and take off. Be prepared."

Ben frowned at the red sports car. "How are we all going to get into that thing?"

Contreras cocked an eyebrow and laughed. "Your nephew can sit in your lap."

Savanna went upstairs to scrub off some of her makeup before lunch. It was making her face itch.

While she scrubbed, she thought about the best way to take the plane. She'd noticed that there were no lights on the runway, so except in a dire emergency, she'd prefer daylight. But not too light. The best time would be dawn.

A couple of hours before sunrise she would drive the Jeep to a spot near the gate and hike the rest of the way to the landing strip. It was less than two miles, and she would have plenty of time to refuel if she needed to and be ready to roll as soon as she could see clearly.

And she'd have to remember to write a note for Father Alphonso telling him where he could find the Jeep. She would leave it downstairs for Juan to deliver.

And Ben. Should she tell him she was leaving?

No. It was her policy never to tell anyone anything before she repossessed a plane.

But she hated to leave without saying good-bye.

Oh, well, she'd think about that later. Tonight was their last night together for sure, and she had plans. She'd seen a killer of a dress at the little shop on the plaza. After an evening of her and that dress, Ben Favor wouldn't kiss her at the door, then go traipsing downstairs for a beer.

EIGHT

When Savanna opened the door, Ben's jaw dropped a foot. He tried to say something, but his vocal cords wouldn't work. He could only stand there and stare at her. His eyes worked just fine. And they seemed to be directly attached to another part of his anatomy, which was also coming to attention.

She wore a white dress that molded her body like shrink wrap. It had two tiny straps and a slit that ran from knee to forever up the side of her leg. She couldn't have been wearing any underwear; he didn't see a sign of a line. But he saw the shadowy swell at the juncture of her thighs, the indentation of her navel, and the sharp definition of her nipples.

Shrugging back one shoulder, she made a sexy little wiggle and ran a hand over the curve of her hip. "Like my new dress?"

Ben cleared his throat. Twice. "Very nice. What there is of it. You're not going to wear *that* downstairs, are you?"

"You think it's too short?"

He glanced at the hem, which skimmed the tops of her knees. "The length is not the problem." He cleared his throat again.

"Then what's the problem?" She wiggled again and looked amused. Ben would have sworn that she was getting a kick out of his discomfort.

"Hell, Savanna, if you wear that dress downstairs, every man in the cantina will go into cardiac arrest. Either that, or they'll consider it an open invitation, and I'll have to beat the crap out of them if they make lewd gestures."

She chuckled. "We can't have that, can we? Perhaps I'd better wear the duster."

When she turned and walked toward her bed, Ben stifled a groan. The damned dress didn't have a back. It dipped so low that he could almost see the dimples on her butt. He knew one thing for damned sure. No, two things. She had a *fine* derriere, and she definitely wasn't wearing underwear.

She slipped on a loose, gauzy coatlike thing that flowed to the hem of her dress. Its big sleeves came to her elbows, and it was white, too, and embroidered with more white. She looked as demure as an angel.

"Better?" she asked.

"For me? No. But the wives and children of Tres Lunas thank you."

Savanna felt very smug as Ben seated her at the table in the courtyard. Just seeing the expression on his face had been worth every penny she'd paid for the dress—even if she had stretched her Visa to the limit. She was surprised to find such upscale clothes in the little shop. It seemed that they kept a stock for the wealthy ladies who came with their husbands to see the bulls at Don Luna's.

Shoes had been a problem. She'd finally settled for a pair of white strappy sandals with a small heel. Ben hadn't even noticed her shoes. She smiled. Who cared? He was looking as her as if he could eat her with a spoon.

She sipped her apple juice, toyed with the gold hoop in her left ear, and basked in his attention.

If possible, the night, the meal, the music, seemed even more romantic than the night before. Rose scents from the centerpiece mingled with warm candle wax and drifted upward. Stars, unobstructed by the lattice, filled the sky.

They didn't talk much as they ate. In fact, Savanna couldn't have told anyone exactly what they had for dinner. Ben didn't seem to concentrate much on his food either; he looked at her more than at his plate.

Dear Lord, she was attracted to him. Wanted him. Ached from it.

She slipped off a sandal and stroked the side of his calf with her toes. He sucked a breath through his teeth. She smiled. He shifted his foot and pulled his leg back. She stroked his other leg.

"Darlin', you're making things very hard for me," he said.

She kept stroking. "How about dessert?"

"Just set a match to me."

The air around them vibrated with sexual awareness, pulsated like a living thing, and heated her skin. She shrugged off her duster, and it fell over the back of her chair. She leaned forward on her elbows and toyed with the stem of her glass. Glancing up, she noted with immense satisfaction that his eyes weren't on her face. They were focused lower.

She knew exactly where he was looking. Hadn't she practiced in front of the mirror? It was her last night with him, and she was going for broke.

From the expression on his face and the grip on his wineglass, she knew that he wouldn't spend his time drinking beer with the boys tonight.

She rose and stretched, every movement exaggerated.

The stem of his glass snapped.

"Did you hurt yourself?"

He looked puzzled.

She motioned to the broken glass and the red wine spilled on the table.

"Naw." He wiped his hand.

"I think it's time to go upstairs." Catlike, she stretched again, slowly, sinuously.

Jose hit a sour note.

Ben grabbed her duster and crammed her arms in it. He scowled at Jose as they passed by his dim corner. "You don't want to take a walk tonight?"

"Not tonight. I need to get up early tomorrow, and all I can think of is . . . my bed."

"Me too."

"You need to get up early?" she asked innocently.

"I doubt if I'll sleep a wink."

As they climbed the stairs, Ben's hand rested lightly on the curve of her hip. She put a little extra sway in her step.

When they reached the door of her room, Savanna unlocked it. The lamp she'd left burning cast a muted glow inside. The bed seemed to fill the room, beckoning. She turned, looked up at Ben, and waited for him to make the next move.

The move came quickly. His arms captured her, and his mouth covered hers with unabashed hunger. His kiss was hot, wet, and wild. She responded with the same fevered wildness. He pulled her closer, grinding her body against his. Deep primal sounds resonated in his throat and brought matching growls from her as the kiss went on and on.

His hands slid beneath her duster to stroke the bare skin of her back from shoulder to the curve of her bottom. Wanting to touch him, she tugged at the back of his shirt to free it from his waistband.

He tried to pull his mouth away from hers, but she followed him on tiptoe and grasped his neck with both hands. He captured her wrists, and his lips left hers.

His breathing was ragged, and she felt his body tremble against hers. Or was it she who trembled?

He sucked in a deep breath, and his whole body shuddered. He sucked in another. "Good night, darlin'."

"Good night?"

"I'm going now."

"Like hell you are." She grabbed a wad of his shirtfront and dragged him inside.

"You know what will happen if I stay." He took three steps backward.

She smiled and kicked the door shut.

Her duster fell to the floor in a puddle.

He groaned, and took three more steps backward.

She slipped out of her sandals and started toward him.

"You're not wearing anything under that dress, are you?"

"Not a stitch."

"Oh, God," he groaned, and tried to step backward again, but the bed stopped him. "Savanna, honey, I don't want this."

She glanced down at the fly of his jeans. "That's the biggest lie I've ever heard."

"You're making this very hard for me."

Smiling devilishly, she rubbed her breasts against his chest, then touched him intimately. "I'm making it hard for me too."

He grabbed her hand. "Don't do that. I'll go off like a skyrocket."

She reached to pull down the strap of her dress. He stopped her. "Don't," he said.

"Why not?"

"Because I want to. I've wanted to ever since I saw you in that dress. All I could think about during dinner was peeling it down and—"

"And?"

He caught both straps and slowly peeled down the front of her dress until her breasts were bared. His eyes caressed her, then his fingers played over her skin, touching swells, brushing peaks. "And this." He bent and laved her breasts with his tongue, sucked at her nipples with a mouth hot with desire. She threw her head back and savored every delightful touch and taste.

He stripped her dress down farther, his mouth following the bared path. Her knees buckled, and she grabbed his shoulders. The dress fell to her ankles. She stepped out of it, and he swung her into his arms.

"Are you sure you want this?" he asked.

"Very sure."

"Then hold on, sugar, we're gonna fly to the moon."

He laid her on the bed, his eyes watching her hungrily as he began stripping. Boots and clothes went everywhere. When he was naked, he climbed onto the bed and knelt between her legs. His gaze feasted on her; his hands stroked upward along the sides of her thighs, her hips, her waist, then cupped her breasts.

"Dear God, you're beautiful. You've been driving me crazy with wanting you."

He tasted her breasts, nuzzled her throat, kissed her face, until she was wild with longing. "Now, Ben. Please." She lifted her hips and grabbed his buttocks, urging him to her.

He froze, hissed an oath, then sat on his heels.

"What's wrong?"

"I don't have any protection."

She smiled. "Look on the nightstand."

He picked up the package and examined it. "Fluorescent?"

She shrugged. "Free samples. I've been saving them for an emergency.

"Well, this is it." He ripped open the first one he came to, and pulled on a blinding chartreuse.

He kissed her again and tested her readiness. She was ready. And he was about to explode. He lifted her hips and plunged deeply. She cried out and writhed beneath him, sending him into a frenzy. He thrust again and again into her sweet wetness as she ground to his rhythm, crying his name, biting his shoulder.

He managed to hold off until she stiffened, back bowed, moaning, and fluttering with spasms that pulled him over the edge of restraint. He erupted so fiercely that he felt torn apart. When the last flutter and pulsation was spent, drained, he rolled over and lay flat on his back.

"I feel like I've been run over by a tank. Will you marry me?"

She laughed. "Sure. First thing Monday morning."

Turning on his side, he propped himself up on one elbow and drew lazy circles around her navel. "I'm serious. It's not such a bad idea. We're a perfect match. And—"

"And?"

"I think I'm falling in love with you. In fact, I'm pretty sure that I am."

She touched his cheek. "That's very sweet, Ben, but totally unnecessary. We had great sex —no, make that *fantastic* sex—but that's all that it is. We haven't even known each other for a week. In a few days you'll be in Alvin and I'll be in Dallas, and our lives will take different directions. I doubt that a year from now you'll even remember my name."

"Don't bet on it. As soon as I get this mess with Kurt taken care of and you get back to Dallas, I'll call you."

"Yeah. Sure."

"I will. What's your phone number?"

"I'm in the book."

His hand slipped up to her chest, and he stroked figure eights over and around her breasts. "God, I love these. Did I tell you that you have beautiful breasts?" He bent and flicked a nipple with his tongue. "They drive me wild."

She laughed. "I sort of got that impression."

He drew one hard peak into his mouth and nuzzled the soft mound around it. When he heard her quick gasp, he chuckled and let go, then brushed his cheek against the damp place his mouth had been.

"Savanna, I have to tell you something."

"Yes?"

"I'm leaving in the morning." He felt her

stiffen. "I'm taking Kurt home. The arrangements are all made."

"How? When?"

"Money is the how. I'm paying a bundle for Ortiz to commute Kurt's sentence to a 'fine.' Ricardo Contreras was the go-between. He's going to pick us up and fly us to Alvin early in the morning."

Savanna jackknifed upright and spat out a very unladylike curse. "Don't count on it."

NINE

"You're a *what*?" Ben roared.

"A repo woman. I'm here to repossess that slimy little chiseler's Cessna. He's six months behind on his payments to the bank. I've been on his tail for weeks."

"So I can safely assume that your tale about being a botanist was a sham?"

Savanna laughed. "I barely know the difference between a grass burr and a larkspur."

"Dammit, why didn't you just tell me instead of running us up and down every pig trail in this part of the country looking for weeds? After listening to you make up names for plants that weren't even remotely correct, I figured that you weren't a botanist, but I imagined that you were everything from a Texas Ranger to a dope dealer."

She giggled and nipped at his shoulder. "A dope dealer? Did you really?"

"No, not really. But you had me buffaloed. I didn't know what you were up to, but I would have never pegged you for a repo woman. Why did you keep lying to me?"

"I wasn't exactly lying. It's part of my cover. Anyhow, I'm telling you now. I could have kept my mouth shut and left you holding the bag. I'm flying that plane out of here at first light."

"You're a *pilot*?"

"Of course I'm a pilot. How could I fly the plane if I weren't?"

Ben sat on the side of the bed and raked his fingers through his hair. "A *pilot*. A *repo* woman. What a mess."

"Come on. It's not that bad. It just means a slight change of plans for you and Kurt."

"Can't you wait for one day to repossess that blasted plane? Ricardo said that he's returning tomorrow night."

"You can't trust a thing that oily snake says. He's lower than worm dirt. I've seen his rap sheet. Ricardo is a con man. In Dallas he lived off his wife's money and beat the dickens out of her at least once a week. From what I've been able to figure out since I've been here, his father-in-law—Don Luna, I've discovered— put a stop to the cash cow and ordered them home, where he can keep an eye on his pregnant daughter and her purse. I wouldn't trust the asshole as far as I could throw him."

Ben frowned. "A *repo* woman?"

"Yep. That's about the size of it."

"And you can actually fly one of those things?"

"Of course. I've had my commercial license for years."

"And that stuff about Contreras's plane being *soooo* cute and asking about all the little thingies on the instrument panel—"

"Was an act. Part of my cover. I needed to find out where he kept the plane and scout the area." She grinned. "Do you think he suspects?"

Ben shook his head. "Never in a million years. Man, you stung me good. Was everything you told me about your past a lie too?"

Savanna scooted close against his back, wrapped her arms around him, and laid her cheek on the top of his shoulder. "No. It's all true. Everything I told you is true except the part about being a botanist. I swear."

"Hell, I knew from the minute I saw you that you were trouble. This whole mess is nothing but trouble, and I'm hip deep and sinking fast."

She recoiled from him, yanked the sheet off the bed, and wrapped it around her. "Don't get testy with me, Ben Favor. I'm not to blame because your nephew acted irresponsibly or because Ricardo didn't make his payments. I'm just doing my job."

"As a *repo* woman."

Furious with his attitude, she stomped around the bed until she was facing him. Fists on her hips, she yelled, "Don't say it as if I were a streetwalker. I make no apologies for my job. It's a perfectly honest way to make a living, and I'm damned good at what I do."

"Oh, God, Savanna, I'm sorry. I didn't mean to belittle you. It's just that the timing is lousy.

"And I'm still leaving with the plane at first light. If you can ditch Ricardo, you and Kurt are welcome to come with me. I'll drop you off on my way to Dallas."

"How do you propose that I ditch Contreras?"

She ground her teeth and rolled her eyes heavenward. "How should I know? Think of something. Be creative."

"It's a deal," he said immediately.

Her eyes narrowed. "No arguments?"

"Nope."

"You fink! You planned to go with me all along, didn't you?"

"The thought crossed my mind. Come here." He reached for her, but she danced away.

"I'm not in the mood."

He laughed. "Give me thirty seconds, and you will be."

She was.

Shortly after three o'clock in the morning Ben pulled the Jeep to the side of the road. "I don't like this," he said to Savanna. "At least let me drive you to the airstrip."

"Ben, we've been over this a dozen times. The Jeep is noisy. If somebody heard the engine on Don Luna's property and came to investigate, we'd be in a fix. I can walk from here."

"But all that junk is heavy." He gestured toward her duffel and big shoulder bag. "And you've got my stuff to boot."

"No problem. I carry it all the time. An extra shaving kit and a couple of pair of jeans is nothing. It's only about two miles, and I'm in good shape."

He grinned. "I can attest to that." He leaned over and kissed her. "Be careful."

"I'm always careful."

They got out and walked the short distance to the ranch gate. Savanna climbed over, and Ben handed her the bags. She waved and took off down the road.

In a few minutes she heard the Jeep start and rumble away.

With the full moon, it was an easy walk.

Except for the chirp of night insects, everything was quiet. Not even a dog barked.

By four o'clock she'd checked out the Cessna—it was fueled and ready to go—and stowed her gear beside three suitcases already on board. She yawned. She and Ben hadn't had much time to sleep, she thought, smiling.

Deciding to take a nap while she waited, she retrieved her travel alarm from her duffel. The suitcases caught her eye again. Why was Ricardo taking three suitcases? He probably didn't intend to return to Tres Lunas anytime soon.

Curiosity spurred her to look inside.

The largest one was filled with clothes. Ricardo's, she was sure. She recognized his usual silk shirts. The other two were jam-packed with neat plastic bundles. It didn't take a Ph.D. to figure out what was inside. The slimy lizard was running drugs.

She wasn't about to transport drugs. She wrestled the heavy bags, including the one with Ricardo's clothes, out of the plane and arranged them neatly beside the runway. That done, she climbed into the cockpit, set her alarm, and dozed off.

At four-thirty Ben was waiting in front of the hotel, when Contreras walked up.

"Where's your car?" Ben asked.

"Parked in front of the church. You ready?"

"Yep."

They started toward the jail. When they neared, Contreras stopped and led Ben to the shadows of the building next door. "You wait here," Ricardo whispered. "I'll distract Jesus for a few minutes. While we're gone, you get the keys, let your nephew out, and meet me behind the hotel."

"What the hell is this!"

"Shhh. This is the way we're getting the boy out of jail."

"Dammit, Contreras, you told me you had things arranged with Ortiz."

"I had a slight problem. There has been a change in plans. You want your nephew freed or not? This is the only solution."

Ben stood with his hands on his hips, fighting the urge to deck the shifty bastard. What a mess. He didn't want to break Kurt out of jail and have the Mexican police on his tail. But Savanna was waiting at the plane. What choice did he have? Damnation! He took a deep breath. "Let's get on with it."

Ben stood in the dark recess and watched Contreras walk to the jail. In a few minutes he came out with Jesus, and Ben overheard Contreras feeding the guard some line about locking his keys in his car.

As soon as they were a decent distance

away, Ben slipped into the jail, grabbed the keys, and unlocked the door leading from the office.

"Kurt! Kurt!" he whispered loudly as he turned the key in the cell door. He strode inside and shook his nephew. "Kurt, wake up!"

"Ben? What are you doing here?"

"Getting my tail in one hell of a crack, I imagine. We're leaving." He jerked the case from the pillow. "Get your clothes on. Hurry. I'll explain later."

While Kurt pulled on his jeans and sneakers, Ben grabbed what personal belongings he could find, including the medicine Savanna had left, and stuffed them in the pillowcase.

"I don't know where my wallet and my watch are," Kurt said.

"Go look in the office while I lock everything back up." Ben quickly wadded the pillow and a sheet into a semblance of a sleeping body, spread the blanket over it, and locked the cell door. He hurried to the center door, locked it, and hung the keys back in their place. "Let's go," he said to Kurt.

"I found my wallet, but not my watch."

"Ortiz is probably wearing it," Ben said as he cracked the front door to look out. "Run around to the back of the hotel. Keep low and keep quiet. I'll be right behind you."

As soon as Kurt was clear, Ben took off after him.

When they were safely in the shadows behind the hotel, Kurt whispered, "You want to tell me what's going on?"

Ben gave him an abbreviated version of what had happened. "But the double-crossing little snake is in for a surprise," he added, grinning wryly.

The Corvette pulled up, and Ben walked to the driver's side. "What's the story, Contreras?"

"You have the money?"

Ben yanked the door open, dragged Ricardo out, and slammed him against the hood. "I thought you said that Ortiz had agreed to free Kurt if I paid a fine."

Ricardo's eyes grew wide and his chin trembled. "He did. I swear it." He tried to struggle from Ben's grip.

"Hold him, Kurt." Ben picked up a loose brick and spread Ricardo's hand on the hood. "I'm going to break your fingers one at a time until you tell me the truth. All of it."

Ben drew back the brick, and Ricardo began to babble. Ortiz had agreed to release Kurt for ten thousand dollars, but not for another few days. By then Don Luna and Ricardo's wife would have returned from their trip. Contreras wanted to be gone before their arrival. He was tired of Tres Lunas, bored with his life under Don Luna's watchful eye. He planned to take all the money and not come back.

"That's the truth," Ricardo whined. "I swear it on my sainted mother's grave."

Disgusted, Ben said to Kurt, "Find something to tie him up with."

A few minutes later Contreras, bound and gagged, was thrown over the hood of the Corvette like a prize buck.

"What are we going to do with him?" Kurt asked.

"We're going to leave Delegado Ortiz a present."

"But who's going to fly the plane?"

"I'll tell you about that part later. Get in."

They drove slowly to Ortiz's house and quietly dumped Contreras at the *delegado*'s front door. Ben stuffed a fat envelope of bills with a note written on the outside down the front of Ricardo's silk shirt.

"By the way, Contreras," Ben whispered in his ear, "your airplane is being repossessed. You should learn to pay your bills." He smirked and chucked him under the chin. "So long, asshole."

As Ben and Kurt started back to the car, a terrible whooping racket started in town, and Ortiz's lights went on.

Ben cursed. "It's an alarm, let's get out of here."

He drove as if the devil were on his heels,

praying that nobody spotted them and followed.

His prayers were for nothing. Topping a
rise a few miles out of town, Kurt yelled,
"They're coming this way. And I think they're
driving my truck. I recognize the lights on my
roll bar."

"How far back?"

"Two or three miles."

Ben cursed and floorboarded the Corvette.
"When we come to the gate, jump out and
open it, then close it behind us. That will slow
them down some."

Savanna's alarm had gone off twenty minutes before. She'd washed her face with bottled water, then taken a few swigs and eaten a
Snickers bar. They still weren't anywhere in
sight. They should have arrived ten minutes
before. The sun was about to rise. Strapped in
the pilot's seat, she craned her neck, scanning
the road.

Lights! And coming fast.

Preparing for an emergency, she set the
throttle and started the engine.

The Corvette screeched to a stop and Ben
and Kurt were out and running. Ben yanked
open the passenger door and Kurt scrambled
inside. "Let's get out of here!" Ben yelled as
he climbed in. "Pronto."

"Buckle up," Savanna said, "I'm rolling."

She was taxiing to the end of the runway, when a pickup truck came barreling down the road. She ignored it and powered up for a rolling takeoff.

The Cessna was full-throttled when Savanna heard a series of cracks and pings.

"Dammit!" Ben bellowed. "They're shooting at us. Get this thing off the ground."

"We're off. Hang on. I'm climbing." Adrenaline poured through her bloodstream, and her heart was beating ninety to nothing, but Savanna forced her attention to flying the plane.

When they had leveled off and were cruising, she laughed. "Wow! I feel like Indiana Jones."

"Man, that was something," Kurt said from the rear. "You're awesome."

She glanced over at Ben. His eyes were wide; his jaw was clenched; and his fingers were welded to the armrests. He had that green-around-the-gills look again.

"Ben, are you okay? Ben?"

"Huh?"

"Are you okay?"

"I'm fine." He closed his eyes, but his jaw stayed clenched and his fingers kept their grip on the seat arms.

"Who was shooting at us and why?"

Ben didn't say anything. Kurt said, "Must

have been the police. Things went haywire. I guess they haven't found Ricardo Contreras yet." He explained events to Savanna.

"I just hope they didn't hit anything vital," she said.

Ben's head jerked around. "Like what?"

"Like a fuel tank."

"Ohmygod! A fuel tank?"

She laughed. "Don't panic. I can tell from the gauge if we're losing fuel. In any case, we wouldn't drop like a rock. This sweetheart could glide to a smooth landing in a field if we had an emergency."

"A *field*?" He went a shade paler.

"Ben, are you afraid of flying?"

"I fly all the time."

"Then is it because I'm the pilot that you're nervous? I can assure you that—"

"I'm not nervous."

She shrugged. "If you say so."

They had been cruising for over an hour with Kurt chattering and Ben doing his sphinx imitation, when the slight stitch in her left side that Savanna had been vaguely aware of for the past few minutes changed to a dull, throbbing ache. Her hand automatically went to the spot.

It was wet.

She glanced down and saw that blood had

soaked a large spot on her navy T-shirt and her jeans.

She'd been shot!

After a momentary flash of panic she forced herself to stay calm and think. It must have happened during takeoff, but she'd been too hyped up for it to register. And it must be a superficial wound or she would have noticed it earlier.

Despite his protests, she knew that Ben was petrified of the plane—she'd seen enough similar reactions to recognize it for what it was. Maybe small planes frightened him, or maybe it was the idea of her piloting it, but the man was scared spitless. She didn't dare let him know that she'd been shot and was bleeding.

She surreptitiously wiped her bloody fingers on her jeans underneath her left thigh. Casually she said, "Kurt, want to help me navigate?"

"Sure. What do I do?"

"Get my duffel from in back and change places with Ben. Ben? *Ben?*"

He glanced at her.

"Would you change places with Kurt? He's going to help me navigate."

"Change places? *Now?*"

She bit back a laugh. "Now. I promise we won't tip over. Unbuckle your belt and move back to a rear seat."

Reluctantly, he moved. Very slowly.

Kurt scrambled into the front. "Wow! This is fantastic, Savanna. I'd love to learn to fly one of these babies. What do you want me to do?"

She didn't need Kurt to navigate. Her route was well planned and her maps were beside her seat, but she needed Kurt's help. Even though she felt okay except for the dull ache, she figured that she ought to put some kind of padding on her side to staunch the wound.

She glanced back to Ben. He had a death grip on the seat and his eyes were closed. To Kurt she made a shushing motion with a finger to her lips. His eyebrows rose in inquiry. She touched her side and showed him her bloody fingers.

Kurt looked alarmed and opened his mouth to say something, but she shushed him again. "I'm okay," she mouthed silently. Aloud she said, "Open my duffel. Find a pencil and a *pad*. Should be in the side zipper pocket."

Kurt did as she asked. His eyes widened when he pulled out an individually wrapped sanitary napkin—the kind for heavy days. "This?"

She stifled a giggle at his expression, then nodded. "Open it," she whispered. When he did, she whispered again, "Hold the wheel for a minute. Don't move it. Just hold it."

She grabbed the sanitary napkin, then

lifted her shirt gingerly. There was a nasty hole just above her waist. The plane bobbled, and she grabbed the wheel.

"What was that?" Ben asked, clearly alarmed.

"Just a little air pocket. Nothing to be concerned about," she called over her shoulder.

Kurt was staring at the hole in her side, his face as pale as Ben's. "Savanna, shouldn't we land somewhere?"

"Is something wrong?" Ben asked.

"Everything's fine," she said brightly. "We're going to land at a small airport I know near Corpus Christi. To refuel. We'll be there soon."

She scowled at Kurt, who was no more help than his uncle, and whispered, "Hand me another one. Kurt!"

He startled, then grabbed another and held it out to her. His eyes widened at the sight of her bloody hand.

"Kurt!"

He didn't move.

She jerked the pad from his frozen fingers and opened it with her teeth. Keeping one hand on the wheel, she plastered the other pad on her side and tucked her T-shirt in her waistband to hold it snug.

A few minutes out from the small airfield near Corpus, Savanna began to feel light-headed.

For the first time, she admitted that she might have been injured worse than she thought. A peek at the pads confirmed that she was losing a lot of blood. She needed to land. Soon. But she didn't dare attempt an emergency landing in a field. Ben was a basket case already.

She could make it. She *would* make it.

There it was! The landing strip. Thank God.

She did her prelanding check and circled the field. Thankfully, there was no traffic and the wind was calm.

"We're about to land," she said cheerfully. "Make sure that your seat belts are securely fastened and your tray tables are up."

Nobody laughed.

Her landing was as smooth as a baby's bottom. She taxied the Cessna off the runway and stopped. She took a deep breath and rested her head on the wheel.

"Ben!" Kurt yelled. "Do something. Savanna's bleeding to death!"

Everything faded.

TEN

Sweet fragrance filled the air. Savanna opened her eyes and squinted. Everything was white and blindingly bright. She felt as if she were at the end of a very long tunnel. Wasn't this the way near-death experiences were described?

Was she dead?

She didn't feel dead.

Her mouth was dry.

She could wiggle her toes. But when she tried to move her legs, she couldn't. They felt weighted down.

She tried lifting her head, but everything spun around and around, so she nixed that idea. Blinking her eyes to refocus, she looked around and saw an IV drip and tubing.

A hospital. She was in a hospital.

She lifted her head again. The weight on her legs was Ben. He was sound asleep, his cheek on the mattress and his arm over her legs. He looked as if he hadn't shaved in a week.

Her lips and throat were parched. All she could think about was water.

"Ben."

His eyes flew open. They were bloodshot and bleary. "Savanna." He jumped up. "You're awake. Thank God." He ran from the room, yelling for a nurse.

She was still thirsty.

A plump nurse with hair like a peroxided Brillo pad bustled into the room with Ben right behind her. "Finally awake, are we?"

"Yes, we are," Savanna said. "Where am I?"

"St. Mary's Hospital in Corpus Christi. You've been one sick little lady, but you're doing fine now. Just fine." The nurse smiled brightly and took Savanna's temperature with an ear gizmo. "Ninety-eight point six."

"I'm thirsty."

The nurse started to reach for the pitcher, but Ben was already pouring water. "I'll do it," he said, poking a straw into the glass and holding it for Savanna to sip.

"How are you feeling?" the nurse asked.

"Like hell. Tired. Very tired."

The nurse patted her arm. "You rest now. We'll take good care of you."

Savanna had a dozen questions, but talking

seemed to take too much effort. She closed her eyes and drifted.

The room was less bright when she awoke. And the sweet fragrance, Savanna discovered, came from a dozen or so vases of roses—red ones, pink ones, yellow and white ones—and two or three more exotic arrangements.

The IV was still in her arm, but this time she could move her legs.

As she stirred, testing body parts, a woman she hadn't noticed before got up from a chair and came to the side of her bed. Tall, tan, and with beautiful, fashionably cut white hair, she had a kind face and an abundance of laugh lines around her eyes—beautiful eyes, gray-blue with an indigo band.

The woman smiled. "Hello, Savanna. I'm Dorothy Favor, Ben's mother. May I get you something?"

"Water, please. And a thick rib-eye would be nice."

Dorothy laughed and held a glass for her to sip from. "I don't think you're ready for a rib-eye, but I'll try to scare you up some broth or some clear soup." She pressed the call button and told the intercom to bring Miss Smith some dinner.

"Nothing with chicken or eggs."

"They know, dear. It's written on your chart that you're allergic. Ben told them."

Savanna glanced around the room. "Where is Ben? He was here earlier."

"His sister Ellen finally convinced him to go to the hotel and clean up. He hasn't set foot out of this place for three days, and he was getting a bit rank."

"Three days? Have I been here that long?"

Dorothy nodded. "After surgery, you were in intensive care for two days, and they moved you here yesterday. You'd lost quite a lot of blood, and you had an infection. But you're doing just fine now. Luckily both Ben and Kurt are your blood type." She chuckled. "Kurt insisted on donating for you, and that took courage on his part. He can't stand the sight of blood."

"Now you tell me."

"What, dear?"

"Never mind. It's very kind of you to come."

"After what you went through for my boys? Heavens, I was glad to do it. You even have a pint of my blood." She winked and patted Savanna's hand. "Now you're part of the family."

The door opened and Ben strode in. "Damnation! I knew this would happen if I left."

"Benjamin Francis Favor! Watch your language," Dorothy said.

"Sorry." A clean-shaven Ben took Savanna's hand. "How are you feeling?"

"Not too bad. I'm hungry."

"What do you want to eat? I'll get it for you."

"I told your mother that a steak would be nice."

"I'll find one. How do you want it cooked? Rare? Medium?"

"Ben, don't be an such an idiot," a woman behind him said. "She can't eat steak yet." The woman, a younger, more chic version of Dorothy, stepped forward and smiled. "Hi. I'm Ellen Wainwright, Kurt's mother and Ben's sister. I'm very sorry that you were injured, but I'm eternally grateful for your help in getting Kurt out of Mexico."

Savanna smiled. "I'm glad that he's safely home."

"Well, back in Texas anyway," Ellen said. "He's at the hotel with the rest of the family. We'll probably run you crazy with the entire tribe trooping in and out tomorrow, but for tonight we'll be on our way. They're waiting dinner for us." She squeezed Savanna's hand gently. "Thanks."

With some effort Savanna raised her hand and fluttered her fingers as Dorothy and Ellen left. "You're not going?" she asked Ben.

"Nope. I'm staying here with you. Later I'll get something at the cafeteria downstairs."

An aide entered with a tray. Ben helped her set it up and raised the head of Savanna's bed. He lifted the dish covers and said, "Hmmm, some clear brown stuff. Some clear tan stuff. Some red Jell-O. And tea. Looks . . . luscious." He tucked a napkin under Savanna's chin and picked up a spoon.

Ordinarily the stuff probably would have tasted like wash water from sweat socks, but the first bit of broth Ben spooned into her mouth was pure ambrosia.

By the end of her second day of consciousness, Ben was driving her crazy with his hovering. It almost took an act of Congress to get him out of the room to eat a meal or change his clothes. He insisted on sleeping in a chair by her bed and feeding her every bite that she took. His entire family, with the exception of Meg's husband and children and his sister Allison, who, thank God, had stayed in Chicago, had visited in shifts all day.

They were all very nice, but she longed for some peace and quiet and space. She hated being confined to a hospital bed and attached to tubes. And she cringed when she thought of the bill she was running up. It would probably wipe out most of her plane fund.

The Cessna. Dear God, what had happened to it?

"Ben," she asked in a panic, "where is the plane?"

"Don't worry. I arranged hangar space for it at the field where we landed. One of the pilots said he could ferry it to Clover Field."

"Clover Field? Why would I want it there? Ben, that plane belongs to the bank. I have to let them know that I've recovered it and get it to Dallas. It means quite a chunk of change to me. I'm going to need money to pay my rent —not to mention my hospital bill."

"Would you stop worrying about the bill? George, Kurt's father, is taking care of your hospital costs. He insisted. And I thought of Clover Field because it's close to my place, but the guy can take it to Dallas if that's what you want. I'll take care of it. Don't worry about anything but getting well. If I hadn't been such a damned fool, you wouldn't be in this mess. God, trouble follows me like a shadow." He raked his fingers through his hair.

"Whoa. None of this is your fault. Are you—" Her comments were cut short by the doctor on his evening rounds.

"You look considerably improved," Dr. Washburn said. "Let's have a look at my handiwork." He took off the large bandage and poked and studied her side. "Looks good. I think we can get rid of all the tubes tonight, and if you're doing well, we can send you home tomorrow afternoon. If," he said, peering at her over his half glasses, "you have someone to take care of you. It will be at least two weeks before you can begin to resume normal activity."

"She's going home with me," Ben said. "I'll take care of her. Or hire a nurse. Whichever is better."

"I'm not going home with you!"

"Yes, you are."

"I am not!"

"Oh, I don't think she needs a nurse," the doctor said, ignoring her protests, "just someone to fix meals and see that she takes her medicine and doesn't overexert."

"I'll stay in a hotel."

"My housekeeper and I can handle that," Ben said.

"Good, good." Dr. Washburn patted Savanna's shoulder. "Well, young lady, it looks like you'll be going home. I'm sure your fiancé will take very good care of you." With that he was gone.

"My *fiancé*?"

Ben shrugged. "I had to tell them something so I could sign for your treatment."

"I'm not going home with you. I'll stay in a hotel and have room service until I'm able to travel to Dallas."

"Savanna, you wouldn't be in this situation

if it weren't for Kurt and me. I'm going to take you to the ranch and take care of you."

"Ben don't let guilt—"

"Guilt? Guilt has nothing to do with it, dammit! I love you!" he shouted.

"Sure you do."

"You are undoubtedly the most stubborn woman I've ever encountered!"

A nurse came in. "Shhh. This is a hospital, sir."

"Sorry."

"I've come to disconnect all these nasty tubes," the nurse said.

"I'll wait in the hall," Ben said.

"Ben, would you do me a favor?" asked Savanna. "Would you please go to the hotel and get a decent night's sleep? I'm okay, and the buzzer is right here if I need anything."

He argued, but she held firm. With the nurse's assurance that she would look in on Savanna regularly, he reluctantly agreed.

He bent and kissed her cheek. "I'll leave my number at the desk. If you need me, call. Okay?"

She nodded.

When he had gone, the nurse sighed. "You're a lucky woman."

After the nurse had disconnected all the tubes and left pushing the IV machine, Savanna felt much better. Freer. Why, except for a little twinge in her side where the stitches were, she was practically well. She didn't need to go home with Ben and endure his hovering.

In truth, she was beginning to depend on him too much. Spending another two weeks with him would be asking for trouble. It would make leaving just that much harder. She knew that Ben didn't really love her; first it was pillow talk, then guilt that made him say that he did. But the fact was, Savanna was developing a very tender spot for Ben. And for his family. They were nice. Like the family she wished she could have had.

No, she couldn't depend on anybody but herself. She'd walk around a little, get her strength back, then check herself out of the hospital before Ben came back in the morning. She was strong; she could do it. She hadn't had a problem when she'd sat up that day while her bed was made.

The first thing she wanted to do was go to the bathroom. She sat up slowly and swung her legs off the bed. So far, so good.

She stood.

Piece of cake.

She'd taken only two steps, when sweat popped out and her entire body began to tremble. Her knees buckled, and she grabbed the foot of the bed to keep from falling. A stabbing pain in her side almost took her breath away.

With the greatest of effort she managed to

get back into bed. Exhausted, she fell against the pillow.

Okay, so she was wrong. She was weaker than she thought. She would rest awhile and try again in a few minutes.

A kiss on the cheek brought Savanna awake.

"How are you feeling?" Ben asked.

"What time is it?"

"Time for your morning oatmeal." He shook out a napkin and tucked it under her chin.

"It's morning?"

"Last time I looked."

Damn! She'd meant to leave last night. She must have fallen asleep after her second try at the bathroom.

When Ben picked up a spoon to feed her, she snatched it from his hand. "I can feed myself. I'm not helpless." She slapped the spoon on her tray.

"Got up on the wrong side of the bed this morning, did we?"

"We didn't get up on any side of the bed, but that's what I intend to do now. I'm going to the bathroom."

"I'll carry you."

"No, you will not. I'm going to walk on my own two feet." She threw back the covers, stood, and teetered. Ben started to grab for her, but she batted his hand away. He stood back, crossed his arms, and watched her. She gathered the open back of her tacky hospital gown in one hand, took two steps, and felt her knees going. "Maybe you could help me a little."

Seeming to be extremely amused by her predicament, he helped her walk the few steps to the bathroom. She refused to let him past the door.

One look at her reflection was enough to bring a groan. Her hair looked like a hog wallow, and her face was pale and hollow-eyed. She performed her morning rituals as best she could, longing for a shower but knowing better than to try to take one. Since every time she went to raise her left arm she winced, she could use only one hand to do something with her wild mop, but brushing her teeth and her hair made her feel considerably better. It also exhausted her.

When she opened the door, Ben was waiting just outside to help her back into bed.

After she'd eaten every morsel of her breakfast, such as it was, he moved the tray and handed her a box.

"Mom and my sisters went shopping for you last night. They said that you would need to wear soft, loose stuff for a while. I didn't bring all of it, but Mom said that the first thing you'd want to do when you got rid of the tubes was to burn your hospital gown. Here."

Inside the box was a cotton-knit gown, butter yellow and downy soft, along with a yellow and white robe that snapped down the front and a pair of white slippers.

A lump came in her throat, and she rubbed the gown against her cheek.

"Like them?"

"They're beautiful. Tell them thank you very much."

He handed her another box wrapped in pink foil and tied with a gauzy gold bow. "This is from me."

She tore off the wrapping and found an entire collection of Safari, from perfume to bath powder. The lump in her throat grew larger. Tears came in her eyes, and she blinked furiously, but despite her efforts, one or two escaped and rolled down her cheeks.

"Darlin', I didn't mean to make you cry. It's just perfume."

"This is very, very sweet of you, Ben, but it must have cost the world. I can't accept this."

"Sure you can. And if you'll give me all the particulars, I'll tend to calling the bank and having the plane ferried to Dallas."

"Ben, you've done too much. I can take care of it."

An aide stuck her head in the door. "Bath time."

Ben kissed Savanna's cheek. "I know you can, sweetheart, but let me. I like to do things for you. Mom and the others will be here later, and while you're taking your bath and getting prettied up, I can make all the arrangements for the plane and for taking you home this afternoon. Okay?"

She sighed. "Okay." She gave him the pertinent information about handling the Cessna.

As soon as she was bathed and dressed in her new finery, the parade of Ben's relatives started. First came Ellen and George Wainwright and their daughter, Karen. Effusive with thank-yous, they stopped by to tell her good-bye before flying home to Houston.

George also had good news. He'd hired a Spanish-speaking attorney in Corpus Christi who had been in contact with Delegado Ortiz in Tres Lunas. Ortiz had found the drugs at the airstrip, and he'd also found Ricardo Contreras, the money, and the note on his doorstep.

George laughed. "Although Kurt's in the clear now, I don't think he'll be going back to Mexico anytime soon. Contreras is occupying Kurt's old cell, and from what I surmise, his father-in-law isn't in any hurry to get him out."

Ellen kissed Savanna's cheek. "We will never be able to thank you enough. Kurt thinks you're wonderful."

"Where is Kurt? I'd like to tell him good-bye."

"He's staying to help Ben drive you home, then he'll spend a few days with his grandparents. I imagine he wants to wheedle Dad or Ben into giving him a summer job to raise money for a new truck."

After the Wainwrights left, Meg and Ben's parents came.

Wearing jeans, boots, and a cowboy hat, Ed Favor was an older version of his son, except for his hazel eyes, steel gray hair, and the little paunch under his belt buckle. "We rode over with Meg," Ed said, "and we're gonna mosey on home. I expect you'll be seeing more of us tomorrow after you get settled in." He winked at her. "You're looking good. Real pretty. Yessiree. Real pretty."

"Thank you." Savanna smiled. "And thank you, Dorothy and Meg, for the things you bought. I was considering burning that hospital gown."

"Aren't they awful?" Meg said. "And drafty."

Savanna chatted with the three for a few minutes longer, then they left. She really liked Ben's family. They were all so warm, even to her, a stranger. It was a shame that—

She stopped herself. No, she wasn't going home with Ben. She was going to pack her things, call a taxi, and go to a hotel. With an effort, she walked to the closet. It was empty. She looked in every drawer. They were all empty. Everything, except her makeup bag, her hairbrush, her toothbrush, and a few toiletries, was missing. She couldn't even find her wallet or a credit card.

"What are you doing up?" Ben asked from the doorway.

"Looking for my duffel and shoulder bag."

"Why?"

"Because I'm about to call a taxi and go to a hotel."

"Like hell you are!"

"Lunchtime!" an aide said, bustling in with a tray.

At two o'clock the discharge papers were signed, medications and personal belongings were in a plastic bag, and Savanna was being pushed to the hospital exit. Ben, instructions in hand, walked beside the wheelchair.

The automatic doors whooshed open, and Kurt stood outside, grinning.

"What is *that*?" Savanna asked, astounded.

"That's how you're going to Alvin."

"In an *RV*?"

"Yep. Borrowed it from a friend of mine. Kurt went and got it yesterday. It has a bed and everything. You'll be very comfortable. I was going to get an ambulance, but Dad said that those things shake your teeth out." He lifted her and carried her inside. "See? All the comforts of home. Kurt's going to drive, and I'll ride back here with you."

Savanna fell asleep as they drove, and woke up only when Ben touched her shoulder and whispered, "Savanna, honey."

She was still groggy when he gently carried her inside and slipped her between cool, crisp sheets.

"Where are we?" she mumbled.

Warm lips touched her forehead. "Home. *Mi casa su casa*. Permanently."

ELEVEN

Donna, the home health nurse, pulled the final stitch from Savanna's side. "Does that feel better?" she asked, swabbing the area.

"Much. It was beginning to itch like crazy. May I take a real shower now?"

"I don't see why not. But you have to be very careful and not fall. You're still a little weak."

"I'll help her," Ben interjected.

"Good. Make sure to keep the area dry."

When Donna had packed her materials and left, Savanna threw back the covers and stood.

"Where are you going?" Ben asked.

"To take a shower and wash my hair. I can't stand it any longer." She headed straight for the bathroom. Ben was right behind her. "Where are *you* going?"

"To help you."

"But I'm going to take a *shower*."

"I know." He pulled off his boots, and started unzipping his jeans.

"What are you doing?"

"Pulling off my clothes."

Savanna rolled her eyes. "I know that. But why?"

He grinned. "I'm going to wash you and your hair."

"But, Ben—"

He stopped her words with a quick kiss. "No arguments. It's not as if I've never seen you naked." He turned on the water, shucked his clothes, and pulled her gown over her head.

Standing under the spray felt marvelous, Savanna thought. And the notion of having Ben run the soap over her body was—dear God, it was unbelievably erotic. He knelt at her feet and lathered her legs, her thighs . . . and higher. She sucked in a sudden gasp, and he stood and moved upward with the soap. He was very careful of her scar.

And he spent a long time washing her breasts. A very long time. She felt them swell and ache; her nipples hardened. She noticed that his jaws were clenched. She glanced down and saw that he was fully aroused.

Aware of the path that her gaze had taken,

he chuckled. "Sorry. It's kind of hard for me to hide."

"Ben, why are you doing this?"

His expression was achingly tender. "Because I love you."

Oh, dear God, she thought, *I love him too.* No, she couldn't. Impossible. Nobody falls in love so quickly. But if it wasn't love that sent her soul soaring, what was it?

By the time he'd washed her hair, she wasn't sure if the steam was from the water or their heated bodies. She touched him intimately, and he flinched.

"Darlin', don't. You're too weak. We can't—"

"Shhh." She kissed him briefly. "Let me touch you."

"Honey—"

"Let me." She kissed him again.

He groaned, shuddered, and held her as the warm spray cascaded over their bodies.

"Oh, Savanna, I love you so," he murmured.

When Ben came in the back door, he paused only long enough to get a drink of water and wipe the sweat from his face. Then he went searching for Savanna. He found her in the den, sitting in the new recliner he'd bought for her, deeply engrossed in a book.

He simply stood there and looked at her, love swelling inside him. Love so powerful that it made his heart almost burst.

Her hair was freshly washed and shiny, and she wore one of the loose knit shifts his mother and sisters had picked out. Blue. He liked her in blue. Hell, he liked her in everything.

He liked her even better in nothing.

But except for a few kisses, after that day in the shower he'd kept his hands to himself.

It hadn't been easy.

Truthfully, it had been hell. He wanted to touch her, kiss her senseless, make love to her until she begged for mercy. At night he dreamed of making love to her. During the day he fantasized about it. He walked funny most of the time.

They'd spent almost every waking hour of the past two weeks together. They'd played cards, dominoes, Scrabble, and Monopoly; they'd watched TV and played rented movies on the VCR; they'd talked endlessly—to each other and to family and friends who dropped by.

Only when she took an afternoon nap, which he insisted on, had he tended to ranch business. Not a problem really. Breeding season, his busiest time, wouldn't begin again until fall. He had a good manager and hands, and Kurt was helping to take up some of the slack.

He still hadn't told her.

When the subject of his "cattle" came up, he danced around the subject. And he was damned nervous about it. She had assumed that when he'd said he had a ranch, he had cattle or horses. Sooner or later—sooner, he expected, since today was her two-week checkup with a local doctor—he was going to have to tell her about his livestock.

He was scared. Bone-deep, sick-to-his-stomach scared. He knew how she felt about chickens and turkeys and anything with feathers. And he knew why. She had a passel of bad memories associated with them. And if living around a few chickens and a couple of hundred turkeys was abhorrent, how was she going to feel about living around several thousand emus?

That's what he raised on his ranch. Emus. He was the largest breeder of the flightless birds in the state. He'd gotten in on the ground floor when emus were first imported and worked hard for a lot of years to get his business going. Now he made a good living at it. Damned good. Beyond his wildest dreams.

But he hadn't told Savanna. And he'd asked his family not to mention it either. He wanted to buy some time.

"Hi!" he finally said.

She glanced up from her book and smiled. He nearly melted into a puddle.

"What are you reading?"

She showed him the cover. "The latest by Sandra Brown. Your mother brought it over after she finished it. It's good. Really sexy." She wiggled her eyebrows.

He laughed. "My mother is a sexy lady. And speaking of sex, you won't forget to ask Dr. Tanner . . ."

"I won't forget." She glanced at her watch. "My appointment is in forty-five minutes."

"I'm going to take a quick shower, and we can be on our way. If everything checks out okay, how about dinner out tonight?"

She beamed. "That would be great. I'm getting cabin fever."

She walked out of Dr. Tanner's office grinning. She winked at Ben. "Let's go out to eat."

"What did he say?"

"I'll tell you all the details later."

In Ben's Bronco she laughed at the expression on his face. She knew that he was itching for the details.

He started the engine, turned on the air-conditioner, then turned to her. "This is later enough. What did he say?"

"Let's see. He said that he had conferred with Dr. Washburn." She ticked off the comments on her fingers. "He said that I had a lovely scar. He said that I could begin resuming normal activities slowly. He said that he wants to see me again in two weeks." She leaned her cheek against her finger and frowned as if in deep thought. "Let's see. Did I forget anything?"

"Savanna, did you ask him about . . . you know?"

"About . . . you know?"

"Woman! Did you ask him about having sex?"

She laughed. "I did."

"And?"

"I believe his exact words were: 'Don't try hanging from the chandelier for a while, but normal lovemaking is okay.' He said that with everything, I should stop if it hurts, and rest when I'm tired. I like your Dr. Tanner. Now can we go eat? I'm starved."

"Are you in the mood for seafood?"

"Always."

He grinned. "I made reservations at Gaido's in Galveston. We can be there in half an hour."

They had a window table at the restaurant, complete with candlelight, and feasted on red snapper with shrimp and crab sauce. The place was full, yet no one hurried except the waiters. Laughter punctuated conversations around them. While they ate, they watched waves roll in from the Gulf, the water gold-shimmered by the low-riding sun.

Tourists, their skins pink from the day's exposure, were thick on the seawall. Wearing outlandish vacation garb, they rode fringed surreys or strolled along eating ice cream or Sno-Kones.

Savanna felt buoyant, vibrantly alive. She glanced at Ben and laughed for no particular reason.

"I'd hoped it might be a little quieter," he told her. "I should have known better."

"I like it. I haven't been to Galveston for years. I'd forgotten what a fun place it can be."

"If you're feeling okay, we can come back one day next week and do the town."

"Great! I'd love it."

"Savanna?"

"Yes?"

"Uh, I'd like to ask you a question."

"Shoot."

"Uh, how do you feel about emus?"

"*Emus?*"

"Yes. They're sort of like ostriches, except smaller, and—"

"I know what they are. I run across them all the time when I'm working crossword puzzles. A three-letter word for flightless bird."

"How do you feel about them?"

She shrugged. "I've never met one. And

given my feeling about two-legged critters, I'm not likely to. Why?"

"Uh . . . just wondering. I'd like to ask you another question."

"I hope it makes more sense than the last one." She took a sip of her iced tea.

"Will you marry me?"

The tea wouldn't go down.

When she finally swallowed it past the stricture in her throat, she said, "Are you serious?"

"Yep. I was serious the last time I asked."

"But why?"

"The usual reason. I love you, Savanna. Don't you love me just a little?"

She turned her glass around and around, watching the ice cubes swirl against the sides. "I suppose I do, but—"

"Savanna, look at me." She glanced up, and her gaze was captured by the tenderness in his magnificent eyes. "What do you mean, you suppose?"

"I'm not sure what love is. I—I've never been in love before."

"Never?"

She shook her head. "It's scary. I'm ordinarily a pretty independent person. I'm not sure I'm cut out to be Suzy Homemaker." Her stomach felt like a rampage of agitated bees. "Let's talk about something else."

She glanced away, then back at Ben. The

pained expression on his face pierced her heart. Dear Lord, she hadn't meant to hurt him; he was the last person in the world she wanted to hurt. She reached for his hand.

He squeezed her fingers and smiled half-heartedly. "I won't rush you. We'll talk about it another time. How about some dessert?"

She smiled brightly. "Dessert would be good. Something chocolate and . . . totally decadent." She slipped off a sandal and ran her toes over his calf. "Are you in the mood for decadent?"

"Always, darlin'. Always."

She leaned forward, and her toes crept higher. She gave him a heavy-lidded look that promised passion and murmured, "Tonight's the night."

On their way home Ben tried to tell himself to take it easy, but his mind spun erotic scenes of Savanna under him, hot and moaning, and his foot stomped heavily on the accelerator.

Savanna tried to think of something else, but she ached for Ben. Her skin was fevered, her breasts swollen. Although neither of them said a word, sensual awareness crackled between them like a severed live wire, hissing and sparking.

She wiggled in the seat. He drove faster.

Two weeks of abstinence while living in intimate contact had taken its toll. Forget romantic foreplay. By the time they hit the door of Ben's house, they were revved up and ready.

Ben slammed the front door behind him with his foot and took Savanna in his arms. She grabbed handfuls of his hair and brought his mouth to hers, kissing him noisily, greedily. He lifted her bottom, and she wrapped her legs around his waist.

A feral sound ripped from his throat, and he started toward his bedroom. They made it only as far as the couch. Clothes went in a flurry of zips and snaps and rips. With his shirt still on one arm and his jeans half off, he laved and nipped at her breasts, covered her throat with frantic wet kisses.

"Sweet heaven, I love you so," Ben ground out. "Don't let me hurt you. Dear God, don't let me hurt you."

"You're not hurting me. I want you. Oh, I want you. Come here." She urged him to her.

In a frenzied tangle of arms and legs and questing fingers, they rolled until Ben was on bottom. He positioned her over him, and they came together in an urgent joining.

She rode him with an eager abandonment, ravenously taking her pleasure and reveling in the freedom of their position.

Her orgasm came suddenly, powerfully.

She threw her head back and sucked in a shuddering gasp of intense ecstasy. Like an interior earthquake, acute spasms shook her body, contracting and expanding, swallowing her into indefinable bliss, sucking Ben after her with a grinding groan.

Then silence.

The grandfather clock chimed, then bonged the hour. One. Two. Three. Four. Five. Six. Seven. Eight. Nine.

Sweat-slicked bodies stirred, eyes met. They laughed.

"Darlin', you sure rang my bell."

They laughed again.

"I think it was mutual."

"Did I hurt you?"

"No." She laid her cheek against his chest and listened to his heart beating. "Did I hurt you?"

"Not hardly." He wrapped his arms around her and held her close. "But I didn't even get my pants off."

"Because I'm so irresistible."

"Undoubtedly." He stroked her hair. "I love you Savanna. I love you so much."

Seconds passed. Endless seconds.

"And I love you, Ben," she whispered, her voice barely audible.

"Say that again."

"I love you, Benjamin Francis Favor."

He groaned. "I should have known that wouldn't get past you. I could kill my mother."

"Why?"

"What kind of name is Francis to hang on a boy? When I was a kid, I must have had a million fights defending my sissy name."

She rubbed her cheek against the soft, damp hair on his chest. "I think it's a very nice name."

He stiffened and uttered an oath.

She raised her head. "What's wrong?"

"I just thought of something. We didn't use any protection."

This time Savanna uttered the oath.

"Honey, I'm sorry. I just didn't think."

Silence.

She sighed. "It's not all your fault. I didn't think either. We'll just have to keep our fingers crossed."

"Would it be so bad? If you got pregnant, I mean."

Her first inclination was to say that it would be disastrous. She could just picture herself eight months pregnant and trying to strap herself into the cockpit of a repossessed plane. Then a strange feeling stirred in her chest, swelled, and brought tears to her eyes.

"Savanna?"

"I—I don't know. I just can't picture myself as a mother. I've never even had a puppy."

He hugged her close.

❖─────────────❖

It was late when they awoke the next morning. It had been a *very* long night.

Savanna had slept on her stomach, and now Ben rubbed her back with slow strokes. "How about some breakfast?" he said. "Some of Annie's pancakes would taste good."

Annie, Ben's housekeeper, did make the world's best. "Sounds fine with me."

"I'll go put our order in. Want to go for a swim later? I know you've been dying to get into the pool."

She rolled over as Ben stood and pulled on his jeans. "What I'd really like to do is see your mysterious ranch."

His hand paused on the zipper. "Mysterious?"

"It must be. Every time I bring up cows, you change the subject."

"You want bacon?"

"See. You're doing it again."

"Sorry. I'm hungry. My mind is on food right now. You want bacon or not?"

She sighed. "Whatever. Suit yourself."

Ben put on a clean shirt, tucked it in, then stood with his back to her for a long time.

"After breakfast," he said, "after breakfast . . . I'll show you around."

"See, that wasn't so hard, was it?"

He turned and looked at her, his expression solemn. "Savanna, do you really love me?"

She smiled. "I must have told you about a thousand times last night."

"After you've seen the ranch, I'll ask you again."

TWELVE

Eyes wide, her stomach snarled with a backlash of emotions, Savanna stared at the rows and rows of large chain-link enclosures. She swallowed the bile rising in her throat. "Those are . . . those are . . ."

"Emus."

She looked back at the big ostrichlike birds running up and down the length of their pens. "Where are your cows?"

"There are no cows," Ben said quietly.

"But you said you were a rancher."

"I am. I'm an emu rancher."

"How many . . . of those things," she asked, waving her hand toward the pens, "do you have?"

"Counting chicks, yearlings, and breeding pairs, about five thousand."

"Five *thousand*? Five *thousand* of those nasty things in your backyard?"

He sighed. "They're not nasty, and they're not in my backyard. The pens are a long way from the house. You didn't even know they were back here, did you?"

"Well, no."

"Do you want to see the rest of the ranch, or do you want to go back to the house?"

"In for a penny, in for a pound," she mumbled.

"Meaning?"

"Let's see it all."

Ben pointed to a house a hundred yards away. "My manager and his wife live there. And that smaller place to the left is a bunkhouse. Two or three of my hands live there; the others come in daily."

"How many people do you employ?"

"Ten full-time people now. During breeding season we usually double that number with part-time help."

"Why? Can't they breed by themselves?"

Ben laughed. "Nature takes its course pretty well. But eggs have to be gathered, numbered, and put in the incubators. New chicks have to be monitored carefully in the hatchers and brooders. They're over there," he said, pointing to a row of cinder-block buildings. "It takes extra manpower just to ID all the new chicks."

"ID them? Are they issued little plastic cards to wear?"

Grinning, he said, "Sort of. We use leg bands and microchips."

"Microchips? Like in computers?"

"Similar. We insert small electronic chips beneath the skin so that we can keep track of who's who."

She shuddered. "Sounds like something out of a horror movie."

"Not at all. It's state-of-the-art. Want to see the production area?"

She hesitated.

"It's empty now. Breeding season runs from about October till March. The last of the season's chicks are old enough to be in the chick barn or outside most of the time."

She squared her shoulders. "Let's do it."

They walked into an anteroom of the building. Ben started taking off his boots. "Take your shoes off and wash your hands with the antibacterial soap beside the sink. Then put one of these on." He pointed to a stack of paper smocks.

Savanna looked askance. "Are we going to do surgery?"

"No. But this is a closely controlled environment. We try to keep this area as germ free as possible."

When they were rigged out in smocks and paper booties, Ben led her inside the clean and freshly painted area. But clean as it was, there was a faint, lingering odor of fowl in the warm air, one that brought back a flood of unpleasant associations. She clenched her teeth and ignored the churning in her stomach and her rising anxiety.

"What's that?" she asked, pointing to a contraption.

"One of the incubators."

"And that?"

"A hatcher."

She bent over and peered into the glass. A large egg was inside. The largest egg she'd ever seen. It was about the size of a small eggplant and a beautiful deep teal-green color.

"I thought you said breeding season was over. Why is that egg there?"

"Sentimentality on my part. That's Minerva's last egg of the season. Nobody told her it was time to quit, and she produced another egg long after she should have. She's the female from one of my first breeding pairs and still the best producer on the ranch. I have a soft spot in my heart for Minerva and her mate, King John. They're thirteen now." He went over to the hatcher and read a notation by it. "If this one is going to hatch, it should be in the next day or two."

Savanna stared at the single egg. It seemed sort of sad sitting there. Alone in the empty, sterile room. Lonely.

She shook off the odd feeling. Why was she, of all people, concerned about a dumb egg? Good grief!

"Does that conclude the tour?" she asked Ben.

"That's about it."

"Good."

"Are you getting tired?" he asked as they walked back to the house.

"Nope. But I'm hot as blue blazes. Let's go for a swim."

They walked quietly down the path for a while. "Savanna, uh, how do you feel about all that?" He gestured with his head to the ranching operation behind him.

"Honestly?"

He took a deep breath. "Honestly."

"It gave me the willies. I don't like two-legged critters. I told you that. Except for the fact that they don't gobble or cluck or chirp, I don't think I like emus any better than I like chickens or turkeys. Don't expect me to set foot in that place again. I won't."

"Fair enough. No reason why you should."

Ben wanted to ask her another question, but hesitated. He dreaded hearing her answer. When they drew near the house, he found he couldn't put it off any longer.

"Savanna?"

"Yes?"

"Do you still love me?"

"What kind of question is that? Of course I do."

Relief flooded him. "Thank God. I was scared to death that after you . . . well, I was afraid that you'd be upset about the emus."

"Do you expect me to gather eggs or feed them or make friends with them?"

"No, of course not."

"Then I'm not upset. I'll admit that I liked it better when I thought you had a cattle ranch, but as long as they have their territory and I have mine, I can handle it."

He hugged her. "Then we can get married."

"Whoa, pardner." She pushed him away. "I didn't say that."

"But, darlin'—"

"Dammit, Ben, you're like a broken record. I—"

He silenced her with a kiss. After a moment he felt the tension flow from her body. And he prayed that in time, he would win her.

Savanna watched Annie bustle around the den with a dustcloth. A large, rawboned woman who wore her graying hair in a coil atop her head, she had twice as much energy as Savanna on her best day.

"Annie, are you sure I can't do something to help you?"

In her unfailingly cheerful way, Annie said, "Not one blessed thing. You just concentrate on getting well."

"But I am well." When Annie looked askance at her, Savanna added, "Almost. And I'm going crazy with nothing to do."

The doorbell rang and Savanna went to answer it. Kurt stood there, a big grin on his face. He'd dropped in several times since she'd been in Alvin, always with some small gift. She was beginning to think that he had a crush on her. "Hi, Kurt, come in. I thought you were working for your grandfather today."

"I am. Delivering stuff from the feed store. I just stopped by for a minute." He offered her the two books he held and followed her inside. "I thought you might be running out of something to read, and I got these at the drugstore. They're mysteries. You said you liked mysteries."

"I do, thanks."

"Well, I guess I'd better be going. I've got some more feed deliveries to make."

"You need an assistant? I'd be happy to go along and help you."

Kurt looked alarmed. "Lord, Ben would skin me alive if I did something like that. You need to take it easy and heal."

"But—"

"I'll see you later." He beat a quick retreat. She took the books and went out on the patio, but she wasn't in the mood to read. She sighed, propped her chin in her hands, and watched the grass grow.

Savanna tossed the magazine aside. It didn't interest her. There was nothing on TV that appealed to her. She didn't want to go swimming. Annie had the day off, and Ben had gone to town on an errand. Dorothy was at a meeting at the church. Everybody had something to do except her, and she was bored out of her gourd. She wasn't used to sitting around twiddling her thumbs. Being grounded and idle made her antsy.

She loved Ben and enjoyed being with him. But they couldn't stay in each other's pockets twenty-four hours a day. He had a business to run; she had . . . nothing.

Oh, she had keys to one of the ranch pickups, but there wasn't anywhere she wanted to go. If she were in Dallas, she'd be at the airport and strapped in a cockpit in a shot. She missed flying. Missed it the way she would miss an arm or a leg. She ached to be in the air.

If she'd been more domestic, she supposed that she could have found something to do around the house, but she wasn't the type to bake apple pies or knit mufflers to fill up time. Ben's large four-bedroom ranch house, though not ostentatious, was very nice and tastefully decorated in what she supposed was a masculine style, lots of wood and leather and plaid fabrics. And due to Annie's careful housekeeping, not even a speck of dust could be found anywhere. Not that she was into dusting either, but it would have given her something constructive to do.

Restless, she went outside and walked around, intending no particular destination.

For some reason, that lonely egg in the hatcher came to mind. Maybe it was because that at the moment she felt a strange kinship with that egg.

Before she knew it, her walk had taken her down the path bordered with black-eyed Susans and shaded by large live-oak trees. Although it was only midmorning, the day was cloudless and promised to be a scorcher.

At the door of the building where the hatchers were, she stopped and looked around. She didn't see a soul. The workers were probably busy at the pens, which were some distance away. She opened the door slowly and stuck her head in. Nobody was there.

She scrubbed up and put on her Dr. Kildare rig, then pushed open the glass door to the larger space.

The egg sat alone and lonely in the hatcher across the room. She went inside and walked over to it. Propping her elbows on the table, she rested her chin in her hands and stared at the big teal-green egg.

"Hi, there," she said to it.

The egg didn't respond.

"You're not exactly a stimulating conversationalist," she said, then laughed at her own silliness.

Odd that this particular egg didn't give her the heebie-jeebies. Not even a familiar flutter of apprehension stirred in her stomach. Of course, it looked very different from a chicken egg, and the room was bright and clean—not like that dark, nasty henhouse from her childhood.

Maybe, after all these years, her phobia was diminishing. "Wouldn't that be great?" she asked the egg.

The egg was silent and still.

"Is anybody really in there?"

Not expecting a response, she continued to stare at it.

It moved.

No. It couldn't have.

It moved again.

Mesmerized, she watched the egg rock back and forth. It rocked and rolled with gyrations that rivaled Elvis's. Odd noises came from it.

Ohmygod!

She ran to the door, flung it open, and yelled, "Help! Help!"

Nobody came. What was she going to do?

Clutching her head, she ran back to the hatcher. The egg had a hole in it. *Peep, peep, peep.* Her eyes widened as the hole got bigger and bigger and a little beak pecked through. The peeping grew louder. The gyrations increased until it was rocking like crazy.

"*Ohmygod!*" She ran back to the door and yelled outside again. "Help! Somebody. Anybody. Help!"

Nothing.

She ran back to the hatcher. A wet, scrawny chick was kicking with his feet and struggling from the shell. She didn't know what to do.

Was there air in the hatcher? If not, the poor little thing would suffocate.

It flailed around pathetically, trying to get to its feet on spindly legs. Then it stopped and simply lay there as if it were exhausted. Sweet heaven, maybe it was dying! Its big brown eyes met hers, beseeching her to do something.

She ran to the door and yelled for help again. Nobody came.

"Well, hell!"

She marched back to the hatcher, opened it, and scooped the chick out. It wiggled warm and wet in her hands. She grabbed a towel and, very gently, swaddled the chick in it. She held it against her, and the chick cuddled close.

Sitting cross-legged on the floor, she held

the chick for what seemed like an eternity, waiting for somebody to show up. Nobody did.

Finally, she decided that she was going to have to go and get somebody. She laid the chick down in a warm nest and towels. He was kind of cute, she had to admit; he'd dried into a long-legged, long-necked fluff of gray and white stripes with polka dots on his head. When she started to leave, the poor little thing made such plaintive peeping noises and pitiful entreaties with his big brown eyes that she couldn't leave him all alone.

Hands on her hips, Savanna looked down at the newborn emu. "Oh, hell's bells, what am I going to do with you?"

Ben strode to the house, irritated that his business had taken so long. He knew Savanna was getting restless, so he'd planned to ask her if she wanted to drive to Houston for lunch and maybe go to a museum or an Astros game. But it was twelve o'clock already.

"Savanna!" he yelled from the kitchen. When she didn't answer, he walked through the house calling her.

"I'm in the bathroom with Elvis," she shouted back.

The door flew open. "You're *what*?"

She knelt beside the bathtub. She glanced

over her shoulder at him. "Close the door so the heat won't get out. I said that I was in the bathroom with Elvis."

"That's what I thought you said. Where's Elvis?"

"In the bathtub. I turned on the heat lamp and put him on a towel to keep him from slipping around, but he's pooped all over it. What do I do now?"

"Pooped all over—" Ben walked over and peered into the tub, then let out a hoot of laughter. "Where did the chick come from?"

"From Minerva's egg. He was born a couple of hours ago, and I guess you could say that I was the midwife. Nobody was around, and I didn't know what to do with him, so I brought him here. Did I do wrong?"

Not for all the emus in the world would he have told Savanna that she did anything wrong or that the chick might not make it. "I'll take him back down to the brooding house and get him settled in. Why did you name him Elvis?"

"Because he was born rocking and rolling. Lord, I've never seen such gyrations. Isn't he cute?"

Ben smiled, but he was looking at Savanna, not Elvis. "Adorable."

When she squatted down by the little pen in the chick barn, Elvis scurried over, peeping as he did every day that she visited him. Savanna had decided that the baby emu thought that she was his mother.

"Happy birthday, kid. You're a week old today. Ben says that we may have to rename you Elvira."

The chick cocked its head.

Savanna chuckled. "I don't think much of it either. How are things going? Getting enough food and water?"

Elvis peeped.

She felt like an idiot talking to a bird, but today was another one of those boring days when everybody was busy except her. Lord, she was going stir crazy.

Concluding that her conversation with Elvis had run its course, she rose and walked back to the house.

Once inside, she decided to check for messages on the answering machine in her apartment. She'd checked just yesterday, but she had nothing better to do.

The first message was from the telephone company, reminding her that her payment was seriously overdue. If she didn't get home soon and get everything caught up, she would have problems. But it was the second message that set her heart to pounding. One of the banks that she often did repo work for had called.

She scribbled down the number and quickly called them back. Yes, she was available. The Houston area? No problem. She'd get right on it. She made notes of all the pertinent information, then hung up.

"Whoopee!"

Feeling high as a kite, she dug her address book out of her shoulder bag and began calling her contacts. Over the years she'd made friends at most of the small airports in the state and at quite a few in other parts of the country.

After only four phone calls, she'd located that sucker. The Cessna 172 was sitting at Hooks airport at that very moment. She could drive to Hooks, which was a few miles north of Houston, in less than two hours and have the plane in Dallas before the deadbeat knew it was gone. Too, she could stop by her apartment, pay bills, and pick up her mail. Great.

But how would she get to Hooks? Ben was at some kind of all-day meeting, Ed was working at the feed store, and Dorothy was at her church group.

She'd take the extra pickup sitting in the garage. Ben had told her a half dozen times to feel free to do so.

She could probably hitch a ride with one of her pilot friends from Dallas back to Hooks. Or she could take a commercial flight back to Houston and take a taxi back to Hooks to get the pickup. She would be back by the next morning. Or the following day at least.

Hot damn!

Whistling a lively tune, she snatched up a few things, stuffed them in her duffel, and scribbled a note to Ben. She leaned the note against the sugar bowl in the kitchen, grabbed the truck keys, and was out like a shot.

THIRTEEN

"Where in the hell have you been?" Ben bellowed. He looked wild-eyed and furious. "I've been going out of my mind for the past two days."

"Didn't you find my note?" Savanna said, taken aback by his anger.

"Oh, I found it all right. Some kind of gibberish about business and a plane, but what in the hell do you mean, running out like that?" he stormed.

She stormed back at him. "Just a damned minute, Ben Favor, I don't have to account to you for my actions!"

"Like hell you don't! I want to know where you've been. I called your apartment a dozen times and got a recording that your phone had been disconnected. Dammit, didn't it occur to you that I would be worried?"

"Worried? Why should you be worried? For your information, I'm fully capable of taking care of myself."

"Capable of taking care of yourself? Damnation!" He raked his fingers through his hair and held on to his head. "Do you call flying around in one of those death traps, while you're still recovering from a gunshot wound, taking care of yourself? I call it stupid."

"Stupid? *Stupid?* Listen to me: Repossessing airplanes is my business, and it's not nearly as stupid as raising a bunch of dumb birds! While I've been twiddling my thumbs around here, my bills have been piling up in Dallas. I had a chance to earn some money, go home, and pay those bills. The telephone company had cut off my phone, and I got there just ahead of being evicted."

"Oh, God, Savanna, I'm sorry. I didn't realize . . . I would have taken care of those things for you." He moved to gather her in his arms. "Let's not fight."

She pushed him away. "Yes, let's do. I haven't said my piece yet. I despise being yelled at for no reason; I promised myself when I was fourteen that I would never take any guff from anyone again. And I won't. Not from you; not from anybody. I hate being treated as if I were an invalid with no sense at all. And most of all, I hate sitting around here feeling as penned up as one of your emus and bored to death. I am who I am; I do what I do. If you don't like that, that's tough." She tossed the truck keys to him. "Take me to the bus station. I'm out of here." She grabbed her duffle and started for the door.

"I'm not going to take you to the bus station."

"Fine. Then I'll walk."

"Savanna, darlin', be reasonable. It's late and there isn't another bus out tonight. Please, let's calm down and talk this through rationally. I'm sorry that I yelled at you. I ought to have my butt kicked clear to San Antonio, but it's just that I was worried sick. I swear to God that I'll never yell at you again."

She kept her back to him.

"Won't you at least stay until you go back to Dr. Tanner for your appointment? It's only a couple of days, and I know that we can straighten this out."

His apologies were so profuse that she had a hard time staying angry. But what Ben wanted from her and what she wanted from life were so disparate, she despaired at their ever being able to find a common ground.

Sighing, she said, "I'll stay until my appointment with Dr. Tanner, but no longer. In the meantime, I'll sleep in one of the extra bedrooms."

Ben looked crestfallen, but he only said quietly, "If that's what you want."

❖━━━━━━━❖

The night before her doctor's appointment Savanna lay in bed, restless, wide awake. Alone. For the past two days Ben had done everything he could to entertain her. They'd spent a day in Galveston and had gone to the horse races in Houston. Their gaiety was forced. Her leaving hadn't been discussed, but she knew that it hung heavy in their minds.

There was no denying that she loved Ben, but loving him wasn't enough. She knew that he was terrified of small planes—of going up himself or having her go up in one—but if she had to give up flying and try to become the wife he needed, eventually she would die. Or go mad.

She punched her pillow and tried to go to sleep, but she couldn't. She longed for Ben's arms around her, for the warmth of his body next to hers.

One last time. She wanted to make love with him one last time.

She stole from her bed, walked quietly down the hall, and pushed open his door.

"Ben," she whispered.

"Come in, darlin'. I'm not asleep."

She walked across the room and slipped between the covers beside him. "Make love to me, Ben. Make love to me."

He kissed her then, a kiss filled with a universe of tenderness. And he made love to her, long, sweet, achingly poignant love to her. With every kiss, every touch, every caress, he murmured words of endearment. With every gentle thrust, he whispered his love.

By the time they were spent, tears rolled down her cheeks.

"Oh, honey, don't cry." He wiped her eyes with a corner of the sheet. "What's the matter?"

"I love you, Ben. I love you so much. But it's not enough. It's not enough."

"Tell me what you mean."

"How do you feel about my flying, about my job?"

"Truthfully?"

"Truthfully."

He sighed and let his head drop back on the pillow. "It scares me to death. But if you married me, you wouldn't have to do that anymore. Savanna, if you'll marry me, I can give you anything you want. Diamonds, fur coats, Cadillacs, anything you want. Name it and it's yours."

"If I'll stop doing repo work."

Silence.

"What if I asked you to give up your dream, sell your business, get rid of every emu on the place, and raise cows? Would you do it? Would you do it for me?"

He hesitated only a moment. "Yes."

"You're more magnanimous than I am. Flying gave me back my life. It's in my blood; it completes me, brings me a sense of joy and freedom that I can't begin to explain. For years I've dreamed of having my own plane. I've scrimped and saved for a long time to make that dream come true. Even though I enjoy repo work and find it exciting, the reason I do it is to be able to fly and to earn money. I wish I could tell you that I would give up my dream for you, Ben. Oh, how I wish that I could. I love you. But if I tried to give up flying, something inside me would die. I would shrivel up."

He tried to say something, but she stopped him with a kiss. "After I see the doctor tomorrow, I'm going home."

Despite his protests, she rose and left the room. There was nothing more to say.

Shortly after breakfast Ben disappeared and was gone all morning. It didn't take Savanna long to pack. She called Dorothy and Ed Favor and told them good-bye, then went down to the chick barn to say farewell to Elvis.

He came scurrying toward her as soon as he spotted her. *Peep, peep, peep.*

Laughing, she squatted down beside his pen. "Well, kid, I've come to say good-bye."

Elvis cocked his head and batted his big brown eyes. *Peep, peep.*

"I'll miss you too. But the folks around here will take good care of you. Maybe I'll stop by and see you sometime." Tears stung her eyes. "Oh, hell, the truth is, I won't be back, Elvis. You see, Ben and I love each other, but I'd make a lousy wife for him. He needs somebody who can knit and bake apple pies and make pickles. I can't do that kind of stuff, and I don't want to learn. I want to fly."

Peep, peep, peep.

"Yes, I know I'm going to be lonely." She sighed deeply. "But that's nothing new. I've been lonely all my life. Bye, kid."

She rose and went back to the house.

Ben hadn't returned by lunchtime, and by one o'clock Savanna was getting anxious. Her doctor's appointment was at two, and her plane reservation was for three-thirty.

At a quarter of two Ben came barreling up in his Bronco. She was waiting at the door with her bags.

"Hi!" he said, grinning. "Had you about given up on me?"

"Almost."

"Sorry. I was busy." He kissed her cheek, and whistling all the while, tossed her duffel in the truck and helped her in.

His cheerfulness galled her. She'd been moping around all day, sad about leaving, and he was acting as if glad to be rid of her after all.

He'd probably figured out that they'd never make it.

Ben was leafing through a magazine when she came out of the doctor's office. He stood and held the door open for her. "What did Dr. Tanner say?"

"He said that everything looked fine. And by the way, he did a pregnancy test too. Negative."

"Damn!"

"Under the circumstances, I should think you'd be relieved. I know that I am."

He mumbled something under his breath, then helped her in the Bronco.

Neither of them said much on the way to the airport. There wasn't much left to say. And if Savanna had had to talk, she would have probably started blubbering. She hated acting like a wimp.

When they reached Hobby airport, Ben turned opposite the direction of the arrow pointing to departures.

"You're going the wrong way," she said.

"No, I'm not."

He followed the street around to an area where private planes were hangared and tied down, then stopped and got out. "Come on," he said as he held open her door.

Puzzled, she asked, "Why are we here?"

"I want to show you something." Grabbing her hand, he took off at a fast clip toward a Cessna 210 that except for missing bullet holes looked similar to the one she'd flown from Tres Lunas.

When they reached the plane, he stuck his fingers in the back pockets of his jeans, rocked back on his heels, and grinned. "What do you think of this one?"

"I think it's a sweetheart. Why?"

His grin broadened. "If you'll stay here and marry me, it's yours."

Flabbergasted, she gaped at him. "Mine?"

"Yep. It will be my wedding present to you."

"But—but that's blackmail."

"Yep. If the stakes are high enough, I can get down and dirty with the best of them."

"But, Ben, I know what one of these costs. I can't let you buy this."

"Hell, Savanna, I can tell you don't know a thing about emus. Do you know what I've been offered for Minerva and King John?" He gestured toward the Cessna. "Enough to buy this."

"You're kidding." Her heart began pounding like crazy. "You're not going to sell them, are you?"

"Nope. I've got money out the wazoo."

"You're *rich*?"

"Rolling. And I talked to a psychologist

this morning. She said that after a few sessions of hypnotherapy, my fear of small planes would disappear. Hell, in a month or two I might want to take flying lessons myself. Wanna teach me?"

She laughed and threw herself into Ben's arms. "You rogue!"

"Oh, God, Savanna, I love you. Will you marry me?"

"Are you sure you can handle my flying?"

"Do you plan to continue repo work?"

"Not if I don't need to anymore. It's flying I love, not chasing deadbeats."

"In that case, I can handle it," he said.

She smiled. "Then how can I refuse?"

He laughed and kissed her long and hard. "Don't ever scare me like that again. My heart can't take it."

"Ben?"

"Hmmm?"

"Do you think that psychologist might help me overcome my feelings about chickens and turkeys and eggs—and emus?"

He kissed her lightly on the nose. "Funny you should bring that up. I asked her the same thing."

"And?"

"No problem. Piece of cake."

THE EDITOR'S CORNER

Warning: the LOVESWEPT novels coming next month contain large volumes of suspense, heavy doses of hilarity, and enormous amounts of romance. Our authors are professionals trained to provide stirring emotion and irresistible passion. Do try their fabulous novels at home.

A Loveswept favorite for many years and now a rising star in historical romance, Sandra Chastain delights us with a brand-new series, beginning with **MAC'S ANGELS: MIDNIGHT FANTASY**, LOVESWEPT #758. Just when quarterback Joe Armstrong has decided his life is over, the doorbell rings—and a long-legged enchantress makes him reconsider! Annie Calloway insists she isn't a vision or a witch, just someone who cares, but Joe doesn't want his soul saved . . . only a kiss that tastes of paradise. Weaving equal parts heartbreak and humor into a tale of sizzling sensuality and a little magic, bestselling author Sandra Chastain sends a heavenly heroine to the rescue of a wounded warrior who's given up hope.

If anyone knows just how delicious temptation can taste, it's Linda Cajio, who delivers a sparkling, romantic romp in **HOT AND BOTHERED,** LOVESWEPT #759. When he rises from the sea like a bronze god, Judith Collier holds her breath. She'd chosen the isolated Baja village as a perfect place to disappear, but instead finds herself face-to-face with a man whose gaze uncovers her secrets, whose caress brands her body and soul. Paul Murphy makes no promises, offers her only pleasure under a flaming sun, but how can the runaway heiress persuade a tough ex-cop they belong to each other forever? Let Linda Cajio show you in this playfully touching story of love on the run.

No one understands the tantalizing seduction of danger better than Donna Kauffman in **THE THREE MUSKETEERS: SURRENDER THE DARK,** LOVESWEPT #760. Rae Gannon fights back wrenching emotions when she recognizes the man who lay near death in the shadowy cave. Jarrett McCullough had almost destroyed her, had believed an impossible betrayal and shattered her life. But now the untamed mystery man is at her mercy, the air sizzling between them as raw need wars with furious despair. Donna Kauffman demonstrates just how erotic playing with fire can be in this white-hot beginning to her romantic suspense trilogy.

Linda Warren celebrates a love treasured all the more because it has been too long denied in **ON THE WILD SIDE,** LOVESWEPT #761. If she hadn't already tumbled to the track from her horse,

Megan Malone knew the sight of Bill North would have sent her flying! Eight years apart hadn't cooled the flames that sparked between the daredevil jockey and the handsome rebel who will always own her heart. Now, this brash rogue must convince a head-strong lady determined to make it on her own that two hearts are better than one. Praised for her evocative writing, Linda Warren raises the stakes of passion sky high in this wonderful romance.

Happy reading!

With warmest wishes,

Beth de Guzman

Shauna Summers

Beth de Guzman   Shauna Summers
Senior Editor   Associate Editor

P.S. Watch for these fabulous Bantam women's fiction titles coming in October. Following the success of her national bestseller THE LAST BACHELOR comes Betina Krahn's **THE PERFECT MIS-TRESS**: the story of an exquisite London courtesan determined to make a solid, respectable married life for herself and an openly libertine earl who intends to stay single and free from the hypocrisy of Victorian society; recognized for her sweeping novels of the

American frontier, Rosanne Bittner presents **CHASE THE SUN**: Captain Zack Myers joins the army for one purpose only—to take revenge on the Indians who'd destroyed his world, but Iris Gray longs for the power to tame Zack's hatred before it consumes their love—and even their lives; Loveswept star Peggy Webb now offers her most compelling love story yet: **FROM A DISTANCE** spans the globe from small-town Mississippi to the verdant jungles of Africa with the enthralling tale of one remarkable woman's struggle with passion and betrayal. Be sure to catch next month's LOVESWEPTs for a glimpse of these intoxicating novels. And immediately following this page, check out a preview of the extraordinary romances from Bantam that are *available now!*

Don't miss these extraordinary books
by your favorite Bantam authors

On sale in August:

LORD OF THE DRAGON
by Suzanne Robinson

MARIANA
by Susanna Kearsley

LORD OF THE DRAGON

by best-selling author
Suzanne Robinson

The day he was condemned and banished from England, his fellow knights thought they'd seen the last of Gray de Valence. But the ruthless, emerald-eyed warrior had done more than survive in a world of barbaric dangers, he'd triumphed. Now, eager to pay back his betrayers, de Valence has come home . . . only to find his plans threatened, not by another man, but by a volatile, unpredictable, ravishingly beautiful woman. Vowing her own brand of vengeance against the high-handed, impossibly handsome knight, Juliana Welles will do her best to thwart him, to tempt and taunt him . . . until all Gray sees—and all he wants—is her. Yet when a cunning enemy puts their lives in peril, the fearless knight will have to choose . . . between his perfect revenge and the passion of a lifetime.

Juliana threaded her way through the foot traffic on the west bridge—farmers bringing produce, huntsmen, reeves, bailiffs, women bringing dough to be baked in castle ovens. As so often happened, Juliana's temper improved with the distance between her and Wellesbrooke. Once off the bridge, she turned north along the track beside the Clare. She rode in this direction through fields and then woods for over an hour.

Juliana stopped for a moment beside a water-filled hole in the middle of the track. It was as long as a small cart. She remembered splashing through it when she chased after her maid, Alice. A little way off she could hear the stream churning on its way to join the Clare. She would have to turn back soon, but she was reluctant. She still hadn't found the jar containing leaves of agrimony, a plant with spiky yellow flowers. She needed the agrimony, for one of the daughters of a villein at Vyne Hill had a persistent cough.

Clutching her cloakful of pots, Juliana searched the woods to either side of the track for the small white jar. All at once she saw it lying on the opposite side of the path at the base of a stone the size of an anvil. So great was her relief that she lunged across the track. She sailed over the puddle of water, but landed in mud. Her boots sank to her ankles.

"Hell's demons."

Stepping out of the ooze, she picked up the jar, balanced on the edge of the mud and bent her knees in preparation for a jump. At the last moment she heard what she would have noticed had she been less intent on retrieving the jar. Hoofbeats thundered toward her. Teetering on the edge of the mud, she glanced in the direction of the stream. Around a bend in the track hurtled a monstrous giant destrier, pure black and snorting, with a man astride it so tall that he nearly matched the size of his mount. Juliana stumbled back. She glimpsed shining chain mail, emerald silk and a curtain of silver hair before a wall of black horseflesh barrelled past her. An armored leg caught her shoulder. She spun around, thrown off balance by the force of the horse's motion. Her arms flew out.

Pots sailed in all directions. Legs working, she stumbled into mud and fell backward into the puddle. As she landed she could hear a lurid curse.

She gasped as she hit the cold water. Her hands hit the ground and sent a shower of mud onto her head and shoulders. Juliana sputtered and wheezed, then blinked her muddy lashes as she beheld the strange knight. He'd pulled up his destrier, and the beast had objected. The stallion rose on his hind legs and clawed the air, snorting and jerking at the bridle. Those great front hooves came down and landed not five paces from Juliana. More mud and dirty water spewed from beneath them and into her face.

This time she didn't just gasp; she screamed with fury. To her mortification, she heard a low, rough laugh. She had closed her eyes, but now she opened them and beheld her tormentor. The knight sat astride his furious war horse as easily as if it were a palfrey. He tossed back long locks the color of silver and pearls as he smiled down at her, and Juliana felt as if she wanted to arch her back and spit.

Juliana scowled into a gaze of green that rivaled the emerald of the length of samite that draped across his shoulders and disappeared into the folds of his black cloak. It was a gaze that exuded sensuality and explicit knowledge. Even through her anger she was startled at the face. It was the face of the legendary Arthur, or some young Viking warrior brought back to life—wide at the jaw line, hollow cheeked and with a bold, straight nose. The face of a barbarian warrior king, and it was laughing at her.

"By my soul," he said in a voice that was half seductive growl, half chuckle. "Why didn't you stand aside? Have you no sense? No, I suppose not, or you wouldn't be sitting in a mud puddle like a little black duck."

Shivering with humiliation as well as the cold, Juliana felt herself nearly burst with rage. The knave was laughing again! Her hands curled into fists, and she felt them squeeze mud. Her eyes narrowed as she beheld the embodiment of armored male insolence. Suddenly she lunged to her feet, brought her hands together, gathering the mud, and hurled it at that pretty, smirking face. The gob of mud hit him in the chest and splattered over his face and hair. It was his turn to gasp and grimace. Teeth chattering, Juliana gave him a sylph's smile.

"And so should all ungentle knights be served, Sir Mud Face."

She laughed, but her merriment vanished when she saw the change in him. He didn't swear or fume or rant in impotence like her father. His smile of sensual corruption vanished, and his features chilled with the ice of ruthlessness and an utter lack of mercy. In silence he swung down off his horse and stalked toward her. Juliana gaped at him for a moment, then grabbed her skirts—and ran.

MARIANA
by Susanna Kearsley

Winner of the Catherine Cookson Fiction Prize

The first time Julia Beckett saw Greywethers, she was only five, but she knew at once that it was "her house." Now, twenty-five years later, by some strange twist of fate, she has just become the new owner of a sixteenth-century Wiltshire farmhouse. But Julia soon begins to suspect that it is more than coincidence that has brought her here.

As if Greywethers were a portal between two worlds, she finds herself abruptly, repeatedly transported back in time. Stepping into seventeenth-century England, Julia becomes Mariana, a beautiful young woman struggling against danger and treachery, and battling a forbidden love for Richard de Mornay, handsome forebear of the present squire of Crofton Hall.

Each time Julia travels back, she becomes more enthralled with the past, falls ever deeper in love with Richard . . . until one day she realizes Mariana's life is threatening to eclipse her own . . . and that she must find a way to lay the past to rest or risk losing a chance for love in her own time.

I first saw the house in the summer of my fifth birthday. It was all the fault of a poet, and the fact that our weekend visit with a favorite elderly aunt in Exeter had put my father in a vaguely poetic mood. Faced with an unexpected fork in the road on our drive home to Oxford, he deliberately chose the left turning instead of the right. "The road less travelled by," he told us, in a benign and dreamy voice. And as the poet had promised, it did indeed make all the difference.

To begin with, we became lost. So hopelessly lost, in fact, that my mother had to put away the map. The clouds that rolled in to cover the sun seemed only an extension of my father's darkening mood, all poetry forgotten as he hunched grimly over the steering wheel. By lunchtime it was raining, quite heavily, and my mother had given sweets to my brother Tommy and me in a vain attempt to keep us from further irritating Daddy, whose notable temper was nearing breaking point.

The sweets were peppermint, striped pink and white like large marbles, and so effective at hindering speech that we had to take them out of our mouths altogether in order to talk to each other. By the time we reached the first cluster of village shops and houses, my face and hands were sticky with sugar, and the front of my new ruffled frock was a stained and wrinkled ruin.

I've never been entirely certain what it was that made my father stop the car where he did. I seem to remember a cat darting across the road in front of us, but that may simply have been the invention of an imaginative and overtired child. Whatever the reason, the car stopped, the engine stalled, and in the ensuing commotion I got my first watery glimpse of the house.

It was a rather ordinary old farmhouse, large and square and solid, set back some distance from the road with a few unkempt trees dotted around for privacy. Its darkly glistening slate roof sloped down at an alarming angle to meet the weathered grey stone walls, the drab monotony of color broken by twin red brick chimneys and an abundance of large, multipaned windows, their frames painted freshly white.

I was pressing my nose against the cold glass of the car window, straining to get a better look, when after a few particularly virulent oaths my father managed to coax the motor back to life. My mother, obviously relieved, turned round to check up on us.

"Julia, don't," she pleaded. "You'll leave smears on the windows."

"That's my house," I said, by way of explanation.

My brother Tommy pointed to a much larger and more stately home that was just coming into view. "Well, that's *my* house," he countered, triumphant. To the delight of my parents, we continued the game all the way home to Oxford, and the lonely grey house was forgotten.

I was not to see it again for seventeen years.

That summer, the summer that I turned twenty-two, is strong in my memory. I had just graduated from art school, and had landed what seemed like the perfect job with a small advertising firm in London. My brother Tom, three years older than myself, had recently come down from Oxford with a distinguished academic record, and promptly shocked the family by announcing his plans to enter the Anglican ministry. Ours was not a particularly religious family, but Tom jokingly maintained that, given his name, he had little choice in the matter. "Thomas Beckett! I ask you," he had teased my mother. "What else could you expect?"

To celebrate what we perceived to be our coming of age, Tom and I decided to take a short holiday on the south Devon coast, where we could temporarily forget about parents and responsibilities and take advantage of the uncommonly hot and sunny weather with which southern England was being blessed. We were not disappointed. We spent a blissful week lounging about on the beach at Torquay, and emerged relaxed, rejuvenated, and sunburned.

Tom, caught up on a rising swell of optimism, appointed me navigator for the trip back. He should have known better. While I'm not exactly bad with maps, I *am* rather easily distracted by the scenery. Inevitably, we found ourselves off the main road, toiling through what seemed like an endless procession of tiny, identical villages linked by a narrow road so overhung by trees it had the appearance of a tunnel.

After the seventh village, Tom shot me an accusing sideways look. We had both inherited our mother's Cornish coloring and finely-cut features, but while on me the combination of dark hair and eyes was more impish than exotic, on Tom it could look positively menacing when he chose.

"Where do you suppose we are?" he asked, with dangerous politeness.

I dutifully consulted the map. "Wiltshire, I expect," I told him brightly. "Somewhere in the middle."

"Well, that's certainly specific."

"Look," I suggested, as we approached village number eight, "why don't you stop being so pigheaded and ask directions at the next pub? Honestly, Tom, you're as bad as Dad—" The word ended in a sudden squeal.

This time, I didn't imagine it. A large ginger cat dashed right across the road, directly in front of our car. The brakes shrieked a protest as Tom put his foot to the floor, and then, right on cue, the motor died.

"Damn and blast!"

"Curates can't use language like that," I reminded my brother, and he grinned involuntarily.

"I'm getting it out of my system," was his excuse.

Laughing, I looked out the window and froze.

"I don't believe it."

"I know," my brother agreed. "Rotten luck."

I shook my head. "No, Tom, look—it's my house."

"What?"

"My grey house," I told him. "Don't you remember, that day the cat ran onto the road and Daddy stalled the car?"

"No."

"On the way back from Auntie Helen's," I elaborated. "Just after my fifth birthday. It was raining and Daddy took the wrong turning and a cat ran onto the road and he had to stop the car."

My brother looked at me in the same way a scientist must look at a curious new specimen, and shook his head. "No, I don't remember that."

"Well, it happened," I said stubbornly, "and the car stalled just here, and I saw that house."

"If you say so."

The car was running again, now, and Tom maneuvered it over to the side of the road so I could have a clearer view.

"What do you think it means?" I asked him.

"I think it means our family has bloody bad luck with cats in Wiltshire," Tom said. I chose to ignore him.

"I wonder how old it is."

Tom leaned closer. "Elizabethan, I should think. Possibly Jacobean. No later."

I'd forgotten that Tom had been keen on architecture at school. Besides, Tom always knew everything.

"I'd love to get a closer look." My voice was hopeful, but Tom merely sent me an indulgent glance before turning back onto the road that led into the village.

"I am not," he said, "going to peer into anyone's windows to satisfy your curiosity. Anyway, the drive is clearly marked 'Private'."

A short distance down the road we pulled into the car park of the Red Lion, a respectable half-timbered pub with an ancient thatched roof and tables arranged on a makeshift terrace to accommodate the noontime crowd. I stayed in the car, preparing to take my shift as driver, while Tom went into the pub to down a quick pint and get directions back to the main road.

I was so busy pondering how great the odds must be against being lost twice in the same spot, that I completely forgot to ask my brother to find out the name of the village we were in.

It would be another eight years before I found myself once again in Exbury, Wiltshire.

This time, the final time, it was early April, two months shy of my thirtieth birthday, and—for once—I was not lost. I still lived in London, in a tiny rented flat in Bloomsbury that I had become rooted to, in spite of an unexpectedly generous legacy left to me by my father's Aunt Helen, that same aunt we'd been visiting in Exeter all those years earlier. She'd only seen me twice, had Auntie Helen, so why she had chosen to leave me such an obscene amount of money remained a mystery. Perhaps it was because I was the only girl in a family known for its male progeny. Auntie Helen, according to my father, had been possessed of staunchly feminist views. "A room of your own," Tom had told me, in a decided tone. "That's what she's left you. Haven't you read Virginia Woolf?"

It was rather more than the price of a room, actually, but I hadn't the slightest idea what to do with it. Tom had stoutly refused my offer to share the inheritance, and my parents maintained they had no need of it, being comfortably well off themselves since my father's retirement from surgical practice. So that was that.

I had quite enough to occupy my time, as it was, having shifted careers from graphic design to illustration, a field I found both more interesting and more lucrative. By some stroke of luck I had been teamed early on with a wonderfully talented author, and our collaboration on a series of fantasy tales for children had earned me a respectable name for myself in the business, not to mention a steady living. I had just that week been commissioned to illustrate a sizeable new collection of legends and fairy tales from around the world, a project which excited me greatly and promised to keep me busily employed for the better part of a year. I was on top of the world.

Ordinarily, I'd have celebrated my good fortune with my family, but since my parents were halfway round the world on holiday and Tom was occupied with Easter services, I had settled for the next best thing and spent the weekend with friends in Bath. On the Monday morning, finding the traffic on the main road too busy for my taste, I detoured to the north and followed the gentle sweep of the Kennet river toward London.

It was a cool but perfect spring day, and the trees that lined the road were bursting into leaf with an almost tropical fervor. In honor of the season, I drove with the windows down, and the air smelled sweetly of rain and soil and growing things.

My arthritic but trustworthy Peugeot crested a small hill with a protesting wheeze. Gathering speed, I negotiated a broad curve where the road dipped down into a shallow valley before crossing over the Kennet via a narrow stone bridge. As I bumped across the bridge, I felt a faint tingling sensation sweep across the back of my neck, and my fingers tightened on the wheel in anticipation.

The most surprising thing was that I wasn't at all surprised, this time, to see the house. Somehow, I almost expected it to be there.

I slowed the car to a crawl, then pulled off the road and stopped altogether, just opposite the long gravel drive. A large ginger cat stalked haughtily across the road without so much as glancing at me, and disappeared into the waving grass. Three times in one lifetime, I told myself, even without the cat, was definitely beyond the bounds of ordinary coincidence.

Surely, I reasoned, whoever owned the house wouldn't mind terribly if I just took a casual peek around . . . ? As I hesitated, biting my lip, a flock of starlings rose in a beating cloud from the field beside me, gathered and wheeled once above the grey stone house, and then was gone.

For me, that was the deciding factor. Along with my mother's looks, I had also inherited the superstitious nature of her Cornish ancestors, and the starlings were a good luck omen of my own invention. From my earliest childhood, whenever I had seen a flock of them it meant that something wonderful was about to happen. My brother Tom repeatedly tried to point out the flaw in this belief, by reminding me that starlings in the English countryside were not exactly uncommon, and that their link to my happiness could only be random at best. I remained unconvinced. I only knew that the starlings had never steered me wrong, and watching them turn now and rise above the house I suddenly made a decision.

Five minutes later I was sitting in the offices of Ridley and Stewart, Estate Agents. I confess I don't remember much about that afternoon. I do recall a confusing blur of conversation, with Mr. Ridley rambling on about legal matters, conveyances and searches and the like, but I wasn't really listening.

"You're quite certain," Mr. Ridley had asked me, "that you don't want to view the property, first?"

"I've seen it," I'd assured him. To be honest, there seemed no need for such formalities. It was, after all, my house. My house. I was still hugging the knowledge tightly, like a child hugs a present, when I knocked on the door of the rectory of St. Stephen's, Elderwel, Hampshire, that evening.

"Congratulate me, Vicar." I grinned at my brother's startled face. "We're practically neighbors. I just bought a house in Wiltshire."

DON'T MISS THESE FABULOUS
BANTAM WOMEN'S FICTION TITLES